CHRISTMAS BRIDE

LINDA FORD

1

Montana Territory, 1884

*I*t wasn't time. He wasn't properly prepared. To leave now would be foolhardy. But Joshua Kinsley knew he couldn't delay even one more day. Not when a beautiful, vulnerable, defenseless young lady had been brought to the camp. Not to the part of the camp where Josh and four others were kept under constant guard. She'd likely have been safer with them. Weary and weak from being forced to work in the mine, they had little energy left for anything but sleep. No, she was in the cabin where their captor lived.

Josh lay on the cold ground of the cave where they spent the few short hours of the night. To all appearances, he slept. But his mind whirled. It had to be tonight. He rehearsed the plans in his head.

Uproarious laughter came from the cabin where Bull and his friends drank.

Josh shifted. He couldn't see much through the distant, dirty window, but his imagination filled in the details. They'd be wanting to get their hands on the female visitor. Even if she had come of her own free will, it would be frightening to be in that company. But he knew she hadn't come freely. She'd kicked and screamed as Bull dragged her to the house.

He had to get her away tonight. Snores came from the others sharing his quarters. He tipped his head back and snored gently. He half guessed the guard would sneak away for a visit to the house and waited for it to happen. They called the guard Toad because he so eagerly jumped to do Bull's bidding. Toad was a little simple and after two drinks would be passed out.

Toad trotted over to the cabin.

Josh waited, knowing the guard would have one drink immediately and the second in fifteen minutes. It wasn't long before he heard raucous laughter and guessed Toad had slid from his chair in a stupor.

Now all he needed was for the gal to make a trip to the outhouse.

Lord, could you make it happen soon? Guide our steps as we flee. Provide our every need.

His pa would be proud of how he called upon the Lord. It was the way he'd been raised, what with his pa being a preacher. But his current situation had driven the roots of his faith into bedrock.

The door to the cabin opened.

Josh stiffened, waiting to see if the guard would return or…

The wide-skirted silhouette informed him it was the

young lady. She looked to have put on her winter coat. Good. That made things easier. Marginally.

One of Bull's friends stood at the doorway watching and waiting.

Knowing he would be invisible in the darkness, Josh slipped from the cave. Keeping to the deep shadows, he eased toward the outhouse. The supplies he'd been squirreling away were in a secret hollow under a rock. He tied them into a bundle and slipped it over one shoulder. The fur robe, he draped around his neck. Then he waited for the outhouse door to open.

It did. The young lady came out slowly, not in a hurry to return to the house.

At that moment, someone inside the house laughed uproariously and the man watching the outhouse left his post.

Josh couldn't have asked for a better opportunity. He poised behind the door. As soon as she closed it, he caught her around the waist and clamped a hand to her mouth.

She fought like a wildcat.

He dragged her into the bushes behind the outhouse. "Don't be frightened. I'm going to help you get away," he whispered.

"Mmfff." She kicked backwards, bruising his shins. She tried to bite his palm, forcing him to press his hand tighter to her mouth.

"My name is Josh. I'm a prisoner here too. I've made plans to escape. When I saw them bring you in, I decided to help you get away."

She slowed her struggles.

"I mean you no harm, but I expect you know Bull and the others have no such reservations."

At that, she fought even more fiercely.

He continued to move them deeper into the woods, but his struggles left a wide trail to follow. He stopped. "I'm going to let you go. When I do, you will have to make a choice. You can scream and bring them out. You can go back as if you've only been about your business. Or you can come with me. I promise I will do you no harm, but I can't promise it will be easy." He released his grip around her waist, tensed, ready to run if she screamed, then uncovered her mouth.

She backed as far away as the trees allowed and stared at him.

He couldn't make out her coloring in the silvery moonlight, but her eyes were wide, her mouth a furious frown.

"What's your choice?"

"I will not go back there. Two of them have already passed out, but that Bull man was drunk and making lewd remarks." She shuddered. "I'd sooner die in the woods."

"I hope that won't happen. I won't promise anything, but we'll do our best."

"I care not for promises. Of late, I've heard many and only seen them broken. I will never again trust a man."

"I consider myself duly warned. Now let's get going." He led the way through the trees. Every minute he wasn't lifting rocks he had spent studying the area around the mine and knew there was a narrow path behind the outhouse. Late at night he'd often seen wildlife tiptoe along it to the river. He followed that trail.

She came at his heels. "Where are we going?"

"Can't say as I rightly know." They kept their voices low so they wouldn't alert anyone to their presence. Or more correctly, to their absence. "As far and as fast as we can though." He ran headlong into the trees. She padded after him.

Branches caught at his shoulder, and he pushed them aside, held them back for the gal to pass. "Guess I need to know your name." He gave his.

"Katherine. Katie Weber."

"Pleased to meet you." He hurried on, anxious to put as much distance between him and Bull's camp as possible before their absence was discovered.

Snow crunched under their feet. Old snow, crusted over. His breathing grew ragged from exertion. They broke into a little clearing and he stopped to study his options. He looked up and found the North Star. He wanted to go south and east, toward any sort of town. But wasn't that what Bull would expect him to do? So, he decided to go north and west. Deeper into the woods, higher up the mountain.

"We'll go that way." He pointed.

"There's nothing but trees."

"There must be a trail of some sort." He walked along the perimeter. "Yup. Here it is." There were tracks indicating it had been used since the last snowfall.

"At least it isn't snowing," she murmured.

"It would be to our advantage if it was. It would cover our tracks." Without thinking to do otherwise, he prayed aloud. "Lord God, hide our tracks. Guide us to safety."

"You think God will hear you?"

"I know He hears me."

"I suppose that's right. The real question is, will He answer?"

The trail was too narrow for conversation, so he didn't answer.

Bull roared, the sound muted by distance and trees. "Where are you, pretty lady?"

Katie pushed at Josh's back. "Hurry up."

He raced through the trees, ducking under branches, hoping they wouldn't slap her and knock her off her feet. The ground fell away at his feet, and he slid down a slope. She tumbled after him. They scrambled to their feet and looked around. A narrow stream, now frozen over, led through the trees.

"We'll follow that." He caught Katie's hand and they ran along the edge. The ground was rough, and they stumbled repeatedly, but righted themselves and carried on. He didn't know how long they'd been running, but his breath wheezed in and out. A stitch grabbed his side. His lungs begged for relief. But he couldn't stop.

Katie fell. Rather than get up, she knelt there. "I have to rest."

He bent over his knees and sucked in air. In a minute, his lungs functioning better, he straightened and strained for indication of followers. He heard nothing. Dare he hope Bull was too inebriated to follow their tracks? Whether or not he was, he would sober up fast when he discovered the two of them were missing.

Josh looked back on their path. Even Toad could have followed the trail.

Apart from fresh snow, their only hope was to keep going, keep ahead of their pursuers.

He offered her the canteen. He'd stolen it weeks ago

and meant to fill it with fresh water before he ran away. Instead, it had stale water in it. He warned her. "Don't spit it out. It's all we have."

She took a mouthful. "Blah. That's terrible."

He reached into his pack and pulled out two dry biscuits and handed one to Katie. "Eat it. It will give you strength."

She gnawed on it. He chomped the second one. It was hard. But it was food. Of which he had barely enough for one person. And for two? He wouldn't worry about that at the moment.

"Ready?" He held out his hand to her.

She took it only long enough to get to her feet, and they proceeded on, trotting as they followed the little stream. They came to a tangle of fallen trees.

He looked for a way under. There wasn't one.

Climbing over was impossible. And dangerous to try.

"We'll have to go around." The underbrush made the way difficult and slow, but they forged onward. Branches scratched his face and caught his feet, almost tripping him. Snow sifted over him as they made their way through the tangled brush. "Are you all right? It's rough going."

"I'd sooner have a few scratches than what Bull has in mind."

Josh tried to get a bearing on his direction. If he followed the creek at least they wouldn't be going in circles nor would they be lost in the deep woods. He paused, looking skyward. The moon shone overhead, lighting the way. Following the creek was the safest and easiest. They had gone to the right, so he reasoned it was time to go to the left and led them that direction.

They went on and on. Shouldn't they have reached the stream again by now?

KATIE STUMBLED AFTER THE MAN. A stranger who might be offering her escape. Or something worse. But she was willing to risk her life to escape Bull. If the escape turned out to be as bad as what she fled....

Well, after the last few days, she wouldn't be surprised at anything that happened to her.

Her feet tangled in the undergrowth, and she fell flat on her face. She lay there, too weak and spent to get up.

Josh pulled at her. "We have to keep going."

"I know. Give me a minute." Her limbs shook with fatigue. How long had they been running?

Josh straightened. "They might have trouble following us through the trees."

She sat up and looked at their back trail, glistening silver in the moonlight. She doubted anyone would have trouble seeing the bare branches where they had passed. Fear fueled her with fresh energy, and she scrambled to her feet. "Let's go."

They rushed onward. She followed Josh blindly. All that mattered was to keep going, getting far ahead of Bull and his associates.

Josh stopped. She bumped into his back.

She strained for any sound of pursuers. Heard nothing but her own ragged breath. She sucked in air and held it. Her heart thudded so loud she still couldn't hear anything else. She let her breath out in a gust.

Josh still hadn't moved.

"What's the matter?"

"I'm trying to find the stream so we can follow it. We should be back to it by now."

"Are we lost?"

His chuckle was mocking. "Let's just say I don't know where we are or where we are going. But I figure we'll sooner or later reach a town, a homestead, or some sort of shelter. Or…" His voice trailed off.

Katie swallowed hard. She understood what he didn't say. Or die trying. Then she stiffened her trembling limbs. "I'd sooner die out here than face Bull and his friends. Let's keep going."

"I agree. We'll go until we drop."

Katie wouldn't admit she was close to that state now. She had lost all sense of time, but it felt like hours since Josh had grabbed her and offered her some very limited options. "How long do you think we've been running?"

"Maybe two hours. But it's only a guess." He pushed forward through the bushes.

She followed. One more step. One more minute. Another step and another minute until…

"We found it."

Whatever he'd found, he seemed relieved.

He stepped aside so she could join him. "It's the creek."

"So, we aren't lost any more?" She chuckled, understanding he still had no idea where they were.

"At least we aren't going in circles." They walked along the bank of the stream. She wished it was smooth and grassy, not lumpy and rocky, but it was preferable to beating their way through the trees. Formerly, the moon had cast sharp silhouettes of them against the snow, but the shadows had disappeared. She glanced skyward. "It's clouding over."

Josh grunted.

The missing moonlight forced her to concentrate more closely on her footing.

Something tickled her nose, and she swiped it away. It happened again. She realized what it was. "Snow. It's snowing."

He stopped and lifted his face. "So it is. Thank you, God."

His faith came so effortlessly. Hers had once too. When her parents were alive. There was something comforting about hearing the prayer.

"Now they won't find it so easy to follow us," he said.

The snow fell softly like a blessing from heaven. No longer anxious about being tracked, they slowed their steps.

The snow grew heavier. Soon they couldn't see ahead.

"We'll hunker down until it ends." He drew aside some bushes, pushed some of them to the side, and broke others until he'd created a hollow. "This will do. It will help us keep warm."

He backed into the shelter and spread the fur robe he wore. "Come and share the warmth."

She hesitated. The last thing she wanted was to share the tiny space with him. Correction. That was the second last thing she wanted. Avoiding Bull was number one. Still, she had learned her lesson about trusting a man. Never, ever again would it happen.

But now that she had stopped moving, she was growing cold. Swallowing back her fear and suspicion, she crawled in beside him. He drew the fur around her shoulders. It didn't reach around them both, but it was warm from his body. She wasn't comfortable by any means, but she could survive.

He opened the sack he carried and pulled out something. Handed it to her. "Eat it."

"What is it?"

"Pemmican."

She'd heard of pemmican—a traditional native food made by combining dried fruit, dried meat pounded to a powder, and fat. When she'd learned how it was made, she wondered how it tasted. She bit into it. It was cold and a little like biting into a candle. As it warmed in her mouth, she decided it was a *lot* like eating a candle and quite disgusting. "How did you get it?"

"A couple months ago Bull traded for it. He gives us rations so we can keep working. I've been saving some of mine."

"How much?" She hoped he had something else in that pack of his.

He chuckled. "It's the best food I have. And will give us lots of energy. Help keep us warm."

"I understand it's good for us. That doesn't mean I have to like it."

"You might wish I had more before we get to someplace."

She didn't want to think how vague his 'someplace' was, so she changed the subject. "Why are you here with Bull? You don't seem his type."

"I'm not. I'll tell you all about it later, but we need to rest while we can. Get some sleep."

She didn't argue but vowed she would not close her

eyes until she had reached safety. *Please, God, protect me and get me to such a place.*

A smile curved her mouth. Here she was, praying as easily as she once had. It felt good and right. What was it her father had said to her on more than one occasion? Something about faith being strongest when circumstances were hardest. That was certainly the situation at the moment.

Snow continued to fall, covering the hollow.

She might as well close her eyes, as there was nothing to see. The only sound was Josh's slow breathing. He must have fallen asleep.

She wakened, fighting someone. Or at least, trying to. But she discovered she couldn't move.A hand clamped across her mouth, and she grabbed at the fingers. Her legs were curled tight and ached. She tried to kick free, but something held them in place.

"Shh. Don't make a sound. There's someone out there."

The reality of her situation returned in a flash. She was hiding in a bush with a man named Josh, a stranger, who had helped her escape. Hopefully to safety.

She nodded, and he removed his hand.

Every detail of her surroundings flared through her brain. The branches of the bush wrapped about them. The cold pressed into her bottom, but at least she wasn't freezing. Their little cocoon had protected them.

She strained to hear what Josh meant. Heard a crunch, a padding that might have been footsteps. Had Bull tracked them this far?

Heavier footsteps. Perhaps a horse? Had the whole

works of them sobered up enough to follow them? She shivered but not from the cold.

Josh held the fur robe around her and squeezed her shoulder.

"It ain't no use."

She didn't recognize the voice, but who else but Bull and his partners would be out there?

"Can't expect to track 'em in this snow." A second unfamiliar voice. "Still comin' down like a blanket."

"They's prob'ly dead. Or soon will be."

"Yah, we could be ridin' o'er their bodies right now." The horse hooves thudded closer. Something brushed into Katie and Josh's hiding place, dislodging a shower of snow. Some sifted over them. More fell away, opening enough of a hole for Katie to be able to see out. Shadowy figures, one on a horse, stood close enough to touch. Two men she thought she recognized from Bull's cabin, but it was hard to be certain in the snow-dimmed light.

If she could see out, they could see in. Her heart hammered as she waited for them to notice the hiding place.

"'Sides, they would've headed for town, wouldn't they?"

"For sure. Likely Bull has found 'em by now."

"Yah. Let's go back."

Horse and rider wheeled away from the bush. The other man trotted after. "Ya could a brought my horse."

"Quit yer whinin'. It's only a few yards to where he's tied."

Katie slowly released her breath. In a few minutes the pair reached the other horse, yakking the whole time about the injustice of being sent out in such weather.

"Man could die out here. Do ya think Bull would care?"

"Nah, he only wants that gal." The words were followed by an evil laugh that sent goosebumps skittering along Katie's skin. "'Course, I wouldn't mind a bit of fun myself."

Katie listened to the horses trot away.

"We'll wait," Josh whispered. "In case it's a trick to draw us out."

Her heart picked up its pace again. Had they been seen?

Had the pair gone to bring Bull back?

2

The thud of the departing horses faded away. Josh strained to hear anything more. How had the pair not seen where he and Katie hid? Perhaps because inside the bushes was dark enough to hide them. Or God had made them invisible. He didn't care how or why. He was simply grateful.

Beside him, tucked under his arm as he attempted to keep them both warm, Katie shuddered.

Several minutes had passed with no more sounds.

"It seems we're safe for now." He meant the words to be encouraging.

She shifted, though there was little room for movement in their tight quarters. "How safe? What if they come back with Bull? Besides, where are we, and where are we going?"

His chuckle rang with irony. "Your guess is as good as mine. But at least we aren't prisoners any longer."

"Seems to me our prison has grown very small."

He couldn't tell if she was grousing or joking. "It's still snowing."

"I need to get out and..."

He understood. His bladder called for relief too. "Let me go first. I'll break us out of here without soaking us if I can." He wished he could get more assurance into his voice, but how could he with nothing but uncertainty before them? Except for God's guidance, and he didn't mean to forget that.

He punched at the opening the horse had created. Snow billowed down, leaving a gaping hole large enough to crawl through. He did so and turned back to hold out a hand to Katie.

She scurried away into the trees. He went the opposite direction. They met again in front of the opening.

"Now what?" she asked.

"It's morning." He could tell by the white light around them. "I can't tell how late in the day it is. It's still snowing enough to hide our tracks. But we could get lost wandering around in this." He couldn't see as far as the creek, and he knew it wasn't more than a hundred feet away.

"Are you asking me for an opinion?"

"I suppose I am."

She took several steps, tripped over something hidden in the snow.

He caught her before she fell. "If this indicates what travel will be like, then we face getting soaking wet from falling in the snow and risk injuring ourselves."

"Then it seems wisest to wait." She looked up to the snow-hidden sky then brought her gaze to him.

Her eyes were blue, he realized. And her mouth set in

a firm line. Perhaps it was always like that, or maybe it was due to the circumstances.

"I agree." What he didn't say was they couldn't wait very long before they ran out of food.

She burrowed back into their shelter, and he followed, brushing aside the snow that accompanied them, and pulled the fur robe across their backs. It didn't reach across their front but had kept them reasonably comfortable in the hours they'd spent there. He wished he had a way of knowing how many hours had passed since they'd fled.

"You hungry?" he asked.

"About hungry enough to eat the bark off the trees."

He handed her the canteen. "Only a swallow or two."

She tipped the canteen to her mouth and grimaced. "I'm not tempted to take more."

He handed her a biscuit and shared a piece of pemmican.

They ate without speaking. He guessed she was as lost in thought as he was.

She was the one who broke the silence. "What were you doing in their company?"

He gave a bitter laugh. "It wasn't of my choosing any more than yours was."

"What happened?"

"I came west looking for…" He shrugged. "I don't recall. If it was for adventure, I got more than I bargained for."

"In the shape of Bull, I'm guessing."

"Yeah. It was Bull. I had hoped to pan for gold. But all the claims had been taken. I was bemoaning the fact when Bull overheard me. He said panning was no good.

A man had to dig for gold nowadays. Said he had such a mine, and he was hoping to find a partner to help him. Invited me out to see it, and maybe if I liked what I saw, we could throw in together. It wasn't what I had in mind, and I told him that. He said how did I know if I didn't look, so we rode out to see it. When we got here, he and his buddies ambushed me. Took my gun, my horse, my gear. Everything. I was forced to work in the mine." He made an angry sound. "Not as a partner but as a slave." He slumped forward, lost in the misery of what his life had become.

"How long have you been there?"

"I'm estimating about a year. It was the beginning of winter when he shanghaied me."

"A year." She whistled. "Why didn't you try and escape before?"

"You better believe I did. Twice. The first time I got as far as the cabin, and Toad made me go back. The second time I got to the road, running as fast as I could. Bull shot me."

"Shot you? I'm guessing you didn't die?" She half smiled, half grimaced.

"He hit me in the leg." He patted the spot. "Forced me to work even with the injury." It had healed slowly but still bothered him from time to time. Sometimes festering.

"That's brutal. He's not a nice man."

"How did you get to be in his company?" Josh asked.

"Through the deceit of a man I was supposed to marry." Every word was spat out like pieces of bitter fruit.

"I'm sorry. You want to tell me what happened?"

"Nothing better to do, is there?"

He shook his head.

"I came west as a mail-order bride. When I saw the notice from Lambert Phillips, I decided the name indicated a sweet, thoughtful man. And his letters verified the notion. But the letters were all lies. And I was foolish enough to trust him."

"What happened?" Josh asked.

"When I met my groom, he had been drinking and gambling with Bull, giving me serious second thoughts about the agreement between us. But before I could tell him I'd changed my mind, Lambert told Bull they could settle what Lambert owed him." Her breath came in hot puffs, and she glowered at Josh like it was his fault.

"How did Lambert suggest they settle the debt?" He thought he knew the answer.

"He sold me to Bull." She huffed. "Like a cow or a wagon." She leaned over her knees, a picture of dejection.

"They are both truly despicable men." Josh joined her in her state of dejection. "A year of my life gone. Wasted working for that man. My poor parents must be beside themselves with worry."

"Do they know what happened?"

"I had no way of informing them. Before I was captured, I only wrote once always hoping I'd have something special to tell them so I put it off. It's been two years now, I reckon. I need to get back home and let them know I'm alive." He leaned forward to peer out the doorway. "Still snowing heavily." His return to Verdun, Ohio would be delayed a little longer. He sat back. "Are you going home when we get out of here?"

"I have no home." The sadness in her voice made him want to offer some sort of comfort.

Here they were, pressed together like a courting couple, sharing personal details, and yet in many ways, separated by a vast gulf as wary strangers.

"Are you an orphan? I know a bit about that. I have six sisters. All orphaned and adopted by my parents."

"I suppose I *am* an orphan, though I was raised by my parents. My mother passed away this spring. Father, when I was twelve."

"I'm sorry." A thought hit him with enough force his legs jerked, sending a shower of snow over them. He brushed it away. "I don't know if one of my parents has died while I was gone." Even contemplating it left him cold. "I have to get back to them. Make sure they are all right."

"I hope you do, and they are."

"Thanks." How he desired to see his family. How long would it take him to reach the nearest town? And from there make his way back to Verdun to rejoin the Kinsley clan?

For a time, neither of them spoke. But sinking deeper into his thoughts was not a place Josh wanted to go.

"Were there no marriage prospects in your hometown?" he asked.

"I am past marrying age."

He twisted to look at her more closely. "I find that hard to believe."

"I'm twenty-one. Considered an old maid. The decent men were all married. Those who weren't, harbored the notion that I was desperate enough to accept their unwanted advances." She shuddered.

Deciding it was wisest to avoid that subject, he said,"I'm twenty-six."

"It's different for men." She studied him as closely as he did her. "Why aren't you married? Was the call of adventure too strong?"

"Sometimes things don't work out." He saw no point in telling her about his failed romance.

A crashing noise drew their startled gazes to the opening. Snow puffed around their shelter.

"Just snow falling from the branches," Josh said. The fluffy cloud settled. "The sun is peeking through."

"Then let's move." She scrambled from the shelter.

He followed, pulling the robe and sack after him. He straightened, blinking from the bright light. The sun had already passed its zenith in the southern sky. The day was half spent.

"Which way?" she asked.

He studied the snow-covered landscape. "I fear we will run into Bull and his men if we go down the mountain."

"That leaves going higher." She gnawed on her bottom lip. "What will we find?"

"We can hope to find a trapper's cabin." He knew he didn't sound any more certain than she did.

"And if we don't?"

He shrugged. "You want to take your chances at running into Bull, or perishing in the wilds?"

"You aren't very good at offering attractive choices, are you?"

He laughed at her reference to the options he'd presented to her back at the mine. "I confess, my record isn't very good."

"Let's hope by the time we're out of this mess you'll have found some better ones."

He grinned. "I'll do my best."

"Climbing it is." She set her face toward the rising creek bed.

"Better let me break trail." He was stronger, bigger, and had better boots for the job. "I can never understand why women wear such flimsy footwear." At least she had a decent coat. A black woolen one with a hood.

She paused to look at her feet. "It seemed like a stylish choice at the time." Facing him squarely, she lifted her chin. "They'll have to do, won't they?"

His grin lingered. "I'll admit they are better than nothing. But barely."

Laughing, she waved him away. "Let's be on our way."

Smiling to himself, he made tracks back to the creek bank and began to climb. The position of the sun informed him they went west. The snow was deep, and within minutes he was panting from the exertion. He glanced over his shoulder. Katie struggled to step in his footprints, and he shortened his stride. They plowed on for an hour before he stopped for a breather. His leg muscles weren't used to this.

"How are you doing?" he asked Katie.

"I'm coming." She breathed hard. "It's a bit of a challenge, isn't it?"

He refrained from pointing out that the snow grew deeper the more they climbed. Instead, he looked around. "I think we need to choose another route."

She glanced about then met his gaze. "If you see a trail leading us to easier walking, your eyes must be better than mine."

"I wish I did. Just as I wish I knew the countryside better."

"Or had a guide?"

He chuckled. "That would be ideal. And maybe he could bring a couple of horses and some supplies."

She laughed, the sound so soft and musical that he stared at her. Sobering, she grinned at him. "If we're putting in an order, could we ask for a big pot of hot tea as well?"

"I like that idea." Standing there grinning at each other would not make it happen. "There's nothing to do but to choose a direction and go. I think we're more likely to find help, maybe run into a ranch, if we head south. I know there are ranches along the eastern slopes. Even worked on one the first summer I was out here. Hey." Excitement renewed his strength. "Every ranch has line cabins."

"Line cabins? What's that?"

"Little cabins built along the boundary line of a ranch. In the summer, a cowboy stays there and rides the boundary to turn back cows, so they don't wander too far. If I had to guess, I'd say there might be such a cabin in this vicinity."

"Nice to know, but how do you propose we find it?" She waved her arms in a wide circle. "There's a lot of country here. We could be fifty feet from such a cabin this very minute, and how would we know it?"

"You're right, of course."

Her eyebrows rose at his words as if to suggest he shouldn't question her.

He laughed. "If you're so smart, what do you suggest we do?"

"I don't know." Her shoulders slumped. "I confess that every decision I've made recently has led to something worse."

He crossed his arms. Knew his eyes had gone hard. The skin had tightened across his cheeks. He couldn't help but pull his lips back into a disapproving frown. "If you're putting your decision to come with me in the worse category, I did warn you."

"So, you did. And even so, I would make the same decision. Where's one of your prayers when we need it?"

"Right here. Right now." He bowed his head. His first instinct was to remove his hat, but he decided God would understand that he needed to preserve his body heat. "Dear Lord, I know You hear our prayers. Just as You see the entire territory of Montana. You see the cabins, the rivers, and Bull. Please steer him away from us, and please guide us to safety." He silently said 'Amen,' then lifted his head and looked around, aware that Katie watched him.

He didn't move. Just waited, though he could not say for what.

Katie rubbed her lips together. "I might turn into ice while you wait for whatever it is you're waiting for."

"Sorry. Let's follow the tree line. I think if we stay a distance away from the trees, the snow won't be so deep." He set out, hoping his guess of what direction to take was correct and didn't lead them into a blind draw.

Or worse yet, into Bull's arms.

KATIE STRUGGLED AFTER JOSH. He'd shortened his stride, so it was easier for her to step in his footsteps. Even so, it was hard work lifting her feet over the snow, which seemed to get deeper by the minute. She tried to think if it truly was or if fatigue and weakness only made it seem so. Her breath roared in and out. She was warm from the exertion, almost grateful for the breeze that had picked up. She stopped to get her breath and let her leg muscles rest a moment.

Josh stopped too. He peered ahead as if something had caught his interest.

She closed the distance between them and tried to see around him.

He held up a hand to signal her to be quiet.

Tremors snaked up and down her spine. If it was Bull, she didn't stand a chance of escaping him in the snow.

"What is it?" she whispered.

He reached back, offered his hand and, when she took it, eased her forward to stand at his side. He pointed to the trees. At first, she didn't see anything, then a dark shadow moved.

"What is it?"

"An elk. Look at the antlers on him. It's amazing."

The animal lifted his head, giving Katie a good view of him. He was indeed impressive. He either smelled them or sensed danger and trotted off with a rolling sort of gait.

"He'd make a few good meals," Josh said.

Katie pulled away from him. "He's too beautiful to shoot."

Josh took the sack off his back and pulled out

pemmican that he divided between them. "Prefer this, do you?"

She chewed slowly. "Honestly? I can't say I do."

"If we don't get someplace soon, we might have to resort to chewing on tree bark."

The cold deepened as the sun dipped behind the mountains.

"We better find a place to spend the night," Josh said.

"I'd like a hotel with a tub of hot water and fine linens on the bed."

"Sounds good to me. Let me know if you find one. In the meantime, we'll see what the trees offer."

Another night crowded into scratchy bushes did not appeal to Katie, but she didn't see any other option, so she followed Josh to the trees, where he studied them.

"This will do," he said, pointing to a stand of thin trees. "These willows can be shaped." He pushed some aside, pulled others together, and soon formed a shelter. It was roomier than the previous night's but not by much. He scooped out the snow and tramped down the ground, so they had a place to sit then spread the fur. If they did the same as last night, they would sit on a few inches and pull the rest around them.

She crawled in beside him. "I held out hope for a fire."

He pulled the fur around her, securing it as best he could. "I'd light one if I didn't think it would let Bull know where we are." A pause as he stared out from their shelter. "And if I had some way of starting one."

She laughed at his woebegone expression. "We survived one night. I dare say we'll survive another. Besides, it's kind of pretty with the moon shining through the trees. And so peaceful."

They sat in the quiet. She refrained from saying it might even be romantic if not for the circumstances and being with a man she had only met. Yet had spent more time with than any other man apart from her father. She wanted to know more about him. "Tell me about your family."

"Why don't you eat while I do so?" He pulled more pemmican from his sack and a dry biscuit for each of them.

She leaned over, trying to see what else was in there. But could see nothing.

He handed her the canteen. She took two swallows, which did nothing to quench her thirst, and returned the canteen to him. He had to tip his head back to get a drink.

Neither of them mentioned the almost depleted water supply.

Best to think of other things. "About your family?" she prompted.

"My pa is a preacher. A fine one, if I do say so myself. Both he and Ma dedicate themselves to helping others. I'm the only child born to them. I think they were both disappointed when they had no other children, but constantly told us that God had other plans for them. Over the years, my sisters came to them. There were also others who came for a time because of family circumstances then returned home." He chuckled softly. "It was a noisy, happy home." A beat of silence. Two.

Katie waited, thinking he was remembering things and would continue when he'd dealt with the memories.

"Adele is only three years younger than I am. I don't remember when she wasn't in our lives. But I was nine when Tilly was left on the doorstep, and I remember it very clearly. Ma was so excited to have another child and yet sad that Tilly's own mother wasn't able to raise her. She was a tiny little girl with a gentle spirit. I always felt I needed to protect her." He chuckled. "Unlike Flora. She and Eve came when I was twelve—little orphaned girls. Eve was older than Flora. She was six and always seemed to think she had to make sure everything went smoothly. But Flora—" He laughed, again making Katie wish for someone to have that kind of affection for her.

"Flora has red hair. From the time she joined our family when she was four, she was never afraid of any challenge. She followed me around and got into all sorts of scrapes. I remember a time she was maybe eight years old. I was leaving home soon to go to college, so I decided to give her a little treat and told her I would take her for a ride in a little cart I had borrowed. She was so excited to go with me."

Katie heard the fondness in his voice. And something else that she knew was sadness at missing his family. "We'll get out of here, and you'll see them again."

"God willing." He sounded more resigned than hopeful.

"We have a choice here. Trust God or lose hope."

"You're right." His voice filled with humor. "At least we have a good choice to choose this time."

Pleased that she had helped lighten his mood, she begged him to finish his story.

"We went out to the countryside, away from the city. I showed her how to skip rocks. We chased a crow, laughing when it squawked and finally flew away. We played tag through a bunch of trees then laid on the grass and looked at the clouds. It was so much fun. I realized then how much I was going to miss her...all of them. I love my parents and my little sisters. I know they are worried about me."

"We *will* get back. I refuse to believe otherwise."

"Thank you for your faith."

The night deepened around them. She was weary from the strenuousness of the day but didn't feel like sleeping. It seemed Josh didn't either, for they both sat upright, leaning over their knees as they looked out at the moonlit landscape.

"Tell me about your family," Josh said.

"I grew up in Jefferson City, Missouri, an only child and well-loved." Thinking he might think it was a lonely life, she added, "I never felt lonely, because my parents and I were close. I remember one time." Her words caught as her throat tightened at the memory. "We were on a picnic by the river, just the three of us, and I was playing on the rocks along the edge of the water. I slipped and fell in. I panicked when I couldn't get my feet under me. Father reached out and plucked me from the water. He said he would always take care of me. I knew he would. I felt so safe." She clung to the feeling the story had refreshed. "Even in his death, he took care of us. He left the house paid for and enough money that we could live in comfort. I didn't have to try and support us, which was a good thing. But Mother began to fail. By the time I was sixteen, I was taking care of her full time. I loved every minute with her." She couldn't go on as she choked up with sorrow.

Josh squeezed her mittened hand. "You've suffered a great loss. I'm so sorry."

She let herself draw comfort from his words and touch. "I ought to have been content to live in the house as an old maid. I might have if two men in town hadn't grown annoying and inappropriate." They'd made it perfectly clear that she should be grateful for their attention.

She wasn't. And then they grew more aggressive.

His hand tightened on hers. "You needed a big brother to teach those two some manners."

His idea tickled her, and she chuckled. "I can picture you protecting one of your sisters. You'd grab the offender by the scruff of his neck and shake him."

"And I'd warn him of all kinds of disasters if he didn't cease and desist."

They both laughed.

It might be nice to have someone stand up for her, Katie decided.

"So that's why you decided to find a mail-order marriage?"

"Partly. But I'd always wanted to marry and have a home and family like I grew up in. A man who would protect and provide, and children to love and nurture."

"A happy, loving home. Like yours and mine."

Katie leaned further over her knees. She might think of going to sleep now.

A snarling growl rent the air. So close, Katie feared whatever it was stood right behind them. Her heart leapt inside her chest.

3

"What was that?" Katie's whisper was hoarse. Although they were already pressed together in the small quarters, she clutched at Josh's arms and held them in a vise-like grip.

"I believe it's a mountain lion."

The sound came again, raising the hair on Josh's arms.

"It's close." Her words were but a breath. "Will it kill us?"

"I hope not." He pressed his cheek to her head and held her tight. He wasn't her father nor a brother, but he meant to guard and protect her every bit as much as if she were Flora or any of the others. Stories he'd heard about the big cats raced through his head.

Toad liked to talk while he guarded them and had an endless supply of gruesome tales. One that blared through Josh's mind was of a woman attacked while working in her garden. According to Toad, the big cat had crushed her scalp before it ripped her to shreds.

Josh shuddered. His mouth close to Katie's ear, he prayed, "Lord God, be our shield and defender."

The snarl came again. Josh tipped his head upward, half expecting the cat to pounce on them. He couldn't make out anything through the shelter of the willows and prayed the animal wasn't stalking them.

He waited, his arms around Katie. If the cat attacked, it wouldn't get her. Not if he could help it.

He strained so hard to hear anything that his ears rang. Silence as deep as a pit echoed around them.

A tree branch snapped. An animal bellowed in the distance. He detected a snarl, but it was further away than the first sound. And then silence returned.

"I think it's gone." From the noise, he guessed the cat had taken an elk. "We're safe." He eased his hold on her, but she clung to his coat.

She sucked in a breath like she'd forgotten to breathe and choked. Sobs shook her.

"Katie, we're safe. We're all right." He wanted to promise her they'd reach shelter, safety, and deliverance, but he didn't make promises he couldn't keep.

She continued to cry, gut-wrenching sobs that tore through his chest.

He was at a loss how to soothe her. All he could think to do was hold her and murmur assurances.

She shuddered and sucked in a trembling breath. "I'm cold. I'm weary clear through. I'm hungry and thirsty. Most of all I'm scared." A sob followed her words. "So scared."

"I am too. But didn't you recently remind me that we have to choose to trust?" He knew something Pa would do. Speak the scriptures. "The Lord is my shepherd." He knew the whole Psalm by heart and quoted it, lingering on one verse, repeating it several times before continuing. "Yea, though I walk through the valley of the shadow of death, I will fear no evil: for thou art with me." He spoke the words again and added, "God is our protector."

"Thank you for reminding me." She sounded drowsy.

He glanced down at her. It was hard to see in the faint light of the moon, but she appeared to be asleep.

"Katie," he whispered.

The only response she gave was a deep, slow breath.

She felt safe enough to fall asleep. *Thank you, God, for Your word and Your protection.*

He eased his back against the trees that supported his weight and closed his eyes.

An ache in the leg that Bull had shot in his second attempt to escape wakened Josh. He was instantly alert, something he had learned while in captivity. Toad posed no threat to the prisoners, but the same couldn't be said for some of the other guards. He tensed, ready to leap to his feet and avoid a kick in the ribs, when he realized he was weighted down. And remembered that Katie slept in his arms.

He tried to ease her to the side, worried she might waken and be shocked to be in such a position.

She murmured and burrowed deeper into her coat.

He watched her sleeping. She had a wide mouth and a well-defined nose. Her cheeks were pink, likely from the time they'd spent outside. Her hood had fallen down, revealing tangled blonde hair. He caught a strand that had fallen across her face and drew it back.

Realizing that he was in a compromising position and fearing she would be offended, he shifted, put her to his side.

Her eyes opened, clouded with sleep.

He knew the moment realization hit. She blinked, sat up, and leaned forward to stare out the opening.

"No more cats?" Her voice carried an anxious note.

"No. Just sunshine." It would be hard on the eyes today.

"What's for breakfast?" she asked. "I'm not normally a coffee drinker, but I think I'd like a large cupful of it today. Plus eggs, bacon, and pancakes. That will do for a starter." Her eyes twinkled as she regarded him expectantly.

"Coming right up." He dug in the sack. There was one dry biscuit and a piece of pemmican left. He broke them both in half and handed her share to her. They were burning up far more energy than they were replacing, and now they would have to survive with no rations. There was barely a swallow for each of them left in the canteen.

She considered the food. And let out a long-suffering sigh. "Sir, I believe you misunderstood my order."

"Miss Webster, I would gladly give you what you ordered and a pile of doughnuts and large slices of apple pie if I had them. I tell you what. When we get to a town, we'll order the biggest breakfast we can find."

She bit off some pemmican. "I'm only teasing. I know you're doing the best you can, and I am grateful." She swallowed. "But hungry."

"Me too. Shall we be on our way?"

"We won't get anywhere sitting here, will we?" She ate

the last of her pemmican and crawled from the shelter. She stretched her arms overhead. "At least it's sunny."

He gathered up their few belongings and joined her. He took a good look around, having no desire to encounter a mountain lion. Down the hill, almost hidden in the trees, he made out the carcass of something. The big cat had made a kill. They would stay as far away from that as possible and hopefully keep out of the cat's territory.

They set out in the opposite direction, following the wooded area. He hoped they would find a cabin nearby. He stopped and sniffed.

"Do you smell smoke?"

She turned full circle as she sniffed. "I believe I do." She laughed. "That's good news, isn't it?"

"Excellent news. We just have to follow the scent." Never mind that it might be miles away. It was the first positive sign they'd had in two days, and he wasn't going to ruin it with doubts and reservations and fears that it might be Bull or one of his men. Though what would they be doing this far up?

There was little wind, but what there was came from the south and west. He led them that direction. A thicket of trees blocked their path, and he skirted around them, which took them a couple miles off course. He stopped and sniffed. Nothing. No smoke.

He closed his eyes in frustration. *Lord, I'm trying to trust You, but I confess I am growing concerned we might not make it out alive. Help us. Guide us. Please.*

A verse came to mind. *I will instruct thee and teach thee in the way which thou shalt go: I will guide thee with mine eye.*

Josh smiled. His parents would be pleased to know

their words had proven to be true. They both said that if the children learned their verses by heart that God could bring them to mind when they most needed them.

Katie tried to catch the scent too. "Was it only our imagination?"

"Strange if we had identical imaginations."

Her laugh lacked mirth.

He waved her forward. "Come on. We'll keep going until we smell it again."

"What if we're going the wrong direction?"

"If we don't find it by the time we reach that tree"—he pointed to a big pine—"we'll retrace our steps and start over." If they hoped to find civilization, they needed to head east and south.

"Fair enough."

They pushed through the snow until they reached the tree. They stopped to catch their breath before they both tried to find the smoke smell.

He shook his head.

She shrugged. "Me either."

There was nothing to do but to retrace their steps. In a few moments he stopped. "I smell it."

"Me too."

"It's that way."

They turned the direction he indicated and fought through the snow, stopping often to search for the scent.

Again, they lost it.

"We'll keep going this direction. There has to be something ahead." He plowed onwards, stopping often in the hopes of smelling smoke. But nothing.

"Josh, I have to stop." She bent over, her breathing ragged.

"Sorry, I'm pushing too hard." He wanted to reach the source of smoke. He realized he counted on it coming from a cabin. The hope of a warm fire, warm food, safety, drew him like a magnet. But he must pace himself, and not just for her sake. He had not had enough food to eat for months and had no reserve strength for this journey. Besides, he couldn't assume they would reach the cabin, if there was one, before nightfall. Smoke could drift a long way in the cold, clear air.

She straightened. "I can go on now."

He forced himself to shorten his stride and go slower. His thinking slowed too. All that mattered was putting one foot in front of the other. His head swam. They needed food and water. They had none. He grabbed a handful of snow and sucked it, even though he knew it would lower his body temperature.

They must go on. There wasn't any other option. The trees trembled. He blinked. It wasn't the trees. It was his eyes. He closed them and waited for the dizziness to disappear.

He turned back to check on Katie. She was on her hands and knees, twenty paces back.

He had to keep his wits about him. For both their sakes. He returned to her side and helped her to her feet.

"We'll stop on top of that rise." He pointed. They needed to set small goals to keep themselves going.

Katie nodded.

They marched onward. The hill didn't seem to be getting any closer. And then they were climbing, the effort making his legs burn and his lungs struggle. *Keep going. Keep going.*

They reached the top, which had been blown clean of

snow, and collapsed on the ground. She reached for his hand, and they clung to each other.

Finally, their breathing returned to normal.

"I don't know if I can go another step." Katie spoke softly, apologetically.

"We'll rest a bit then move on." The sun had dipped to the west. Daylight hours were short this time of year. "If we don't locate the source of that smoke soon, we'll hunker down for the night." Would they waken the next morning? He pushed resolve into his soul. He would get Katie to safety if it took the last ounce of his strength.

He admitted he was operating on that last ounce already.

He couldn't guess how long they remained there, but he knew they couldn't stay. Even if there weren't a few hours of light remaining, it was not a good place to spend the night. They needed some form of shelter. Not only from the cold, but from wild animals.

Pushing himself to his feet, he studied their surroundings, searching for a good place.

A flash in the distance caught his attention.

"Katie!" Josh's call roused her from her stupor. He grabbed her hand and pulled her to her feet. She knew she had to keep going, but all she truly wanted was to lie down and rest.

"Katie, look." He caught her chin and turned her the direction he meant. "What do you see?"

"Trees and snow. More trees and snow." It made her weary just to see the vastness before them.

"Look more closely. Between that towering pine and that little dip in the ground."

She squinted. "What am I looking for?"

"A cabin. See it?"

She shook her head. "You sure it's not your imagination?"

"Do you see the twist of smoke?"

"Maybe."

"It's from the cabin. We've found the place."

"How are we going to get there?" It appeared to be a long way off. A long, weary way.

"We'll make it. Come on. It's mostly downhill. We can do this."

"I don't know if I can."

"Yes, you can. You must." He began to walk, waiting expectantly for her to follow.

It was easier to walk than to argue.

"Just think. You're going to get back to civilization. You'll find yourself a decent man to marry and have that home and family you dream of."

His words burrowed into her thoughts and into her soul. They gave her new strength. She would make it out of here. She would marry and have the home she wanted. If she could find a man to trust, she belatedly reminded herself.

An hour later, after plodding through the snow, she seriously doubted she'd live to see that dream come true. The snow was up to her knees in many places. Lifting one foot after the other sucked out what little energy she had left. Her lungs burned from the exertion. She'd opened her coat and thrown back her hood. At the moment, she'd gladly trade her coat for a long drink of water.

She stopped. She couldn't go on.

Josh plowed onward. He rubbed his left leg as he walked. Was that where he'd been shot? Or had he injured it as he broke trail?

He glanced over his shoulder. Saw she wasn't moving. "Katie? What's wrong?"

She gave a snort of laughter. "You mean besides being thirsty, hungry, and so tired I can't lift my feet even one more time?"

"We're almost through the worst part. The rest will be easier."

"I fear you are saying that solely to make me keep going."

His laugh was wheezy from overworked lungs. "Are you saying you don't trust me?"

"I've decided I won't trust anyone. Too risky."

"Then it doesn't matter what I say."

She shrugged. "You seem like a nice enough man. And what with your pa being a preacher, you might be all right. My decision is based on my experiences. Not your upbringing."

"Fair enough. But I'm all you've got right now." He held out his hand.

She shook her head. "I simply can't take another step."

He marched to her side and took her hand, ignoring her attempt to pull away. "We have to go on."

With him pulling her, she had no choice but to comply.

"Look." He pointed toward the cabin which, indeed, seemed much closer. "Do you see that?"

"I see the cabin." Then she saw a flash of light reflecting off something shiny. "Did you see it?"

"Yes." He grinned at her. "You ready to go on?"

"Lead on, brave soldier. Lead on." She could think of no explanation why that flash had renewed her strength and determination, but it had.

After a hundred yards, her strength was spent. "I can't do this," she wailed.

Josh returned to her side and took her hand. "Yes, you can. We're almost there. Think of water to drink. A big pot of tea. And that hearty breakfast you've been hankering after." He pulled her forward as he talked. "See, you can make it."

"I'm all right now." She wasn't really but didn't want Josh expending his energy dragging her along.

"You're sure?"

"Yes, I am. Like you said, we are almost there."

He went ahead again, breaking trail. Limping heavily.

Time had slowed to a standstill. Distance had expanded. Although they kept moving, the cabin didn't seem to be getting any closer. Then the ground rose and required every bit of her determination to keep going.

Josh stopped. She bent over her knees, begging her heart to stop pounding like thunder in her ears. Her breathing slowed enough she could speak.

"Is something wrong?"

"We're here."

Here? Where? Then she lifted her gaze from the ground before her feet. The cabin stood in front of them. Not more than twenty yards away. "We made it. I can't believe it."

The snow in the yard was packed. Josh took her hand and they staggered to the door.

He knocked.

No one came.

"I know someone must be inside," he whispered, then raised his voice and yelled. "Please let us in. We're lost and cold." He rattled the door, but it was barred.

A scuffling made Katie ready to rush inside as soon as the door opened.

But what opened was a slit in the door, and what appeared was the barrel of a shotgun aimed right at Josh's chest.

4

---

*J*osh jumped aside, pushing Katie the other direction. "Don't shoot," he yelled. "We only want shelter."

"Go away. You're not welcome." The words were croaky.

"Why not?" Katie demanded.

Josh could hear the irritation in her voice and signaled with his hand for her to stay calm.

She frowned at him and turned back to the door. "We've wandered in the cold and snow for two days. I'm hungry and thirsty and tired. Couldn't you show us a little Christian charity?"

"No."

"I don't think he wants to negotiate," Josh whispered. He turned to consider if the yard offered any options. There was nothing but a small shed that he guessed served as a place to store wood and other things. He raised his voice. "We'll spend the night in your shed if you don't mind."

"I mind."

"What is wrong with you? We're in dire need. You can't turn us away." Katie's voice was sharp with anger and disapproval.

Josh grabbed Katie's hand and dragged her from the door. She put up a struggle. "Katie, are you trying to get us killed?"

She jerked away from him. "The only thing that has kept me going for the last what seems like a hundred miles was the promise of a hot drink and something to eat. I'm not going to be turned away." She marched back to the door before Josh could stop her.

To her credit, she stood to one side of the gun barrel.

But the man inside shifted so it pointed her direction.

She moved further away. "Have mercy on us. We've run out of food and water."

No answer.

Katie kicked at the door. "Are you prepared to stay there all night listening to my complaints? Because I'm not going to be quiet."

"Suit yourself." The gun barrel withdrew. The little door slapped shut.

Katie screamed. "You're a heartless person. Just as bad as Bull or Lambert."

Silence answered her.

She leaned her forehead against the solid door and wept.

Josh went to her and pulled her into his arms. "We'll be all right. You'll see. Come. Let's make ourselves comfortable in the shed."

She sniffed. "You think there's a soft bed? A warm fire?" She straightened and hollered again at the door.

"Could you toss out a match or two so we can at least start a fire and stay warm?"

"Lambert who?"

Katie glanced back at Josh, surprised by the question. "What difference does it make? He's just another worthless man."

"Answer me."

"Lambert Philips."

"How do you know the man?"

"I wish I didn't."

"Answer me."

She shrugged. "Very well. I came west as a mail-order bride, expecting to marry him. But he turned out to be nothing like his letters portrayed, and then the snake sold me to Bull."

A sound, suspiciously like choking laughter, came from inside.

"It's not the least bit amusing," Katie groused. "And now because you won't let us in, I'm going to perish from cold and hunger. My trip west has been a bitter experience."

"Sorry, but it's not my fault."

Katie drew herself up in indignation. "It's your fault as much as anyone's for not offering us shelter. Can't say as you're much different than Lambert." Her mouth twisted on the man's name.

"I'm not at all like him."

A grating made Josh think the bar was being shoved aside, and then the door opened.

A young man, or rather, a boy of maybe twelve or thirteen, stood in the opening and studied them, the shotgun, resting along his arm, pointed at them. His young age explained his raspy voice. He'd been trying to make them think he was much older.

Josh moved aside so they were a wider target. What was a boy doing out here alone?

The barrel of the gun followed his movement.

"Shed your firearms."

Josh lifted his hands. "We have none."

The boy guffawed. His voice broke, and he cut off his amusement. "Let me get this straight. You're out in the middle of winter without food or a firearm."

"Or water," Katie added.

"And no matches?" It was less a question than an accusation. "Seems pretty dumb to me."

"You do what you have to do," Josh said by way of explanation.

"I know that to be true."

"We decided not to accept Bull's hospitality." Katie's tone of voice made it clear that it wasn't hospitality that Bull offered. "Are you going to let us in or not?" she demanded.

The boy lowered the gun. "I'm only doing it because I won't be accused of being like Lambert." He stepped aside. "'Fraid it's not much."

Katie rushed past him to the stove and held out her hands. "It's the most beautiful place I've seen in many days. Since I sold my own house to come west."

Josh wished her face didn't pucker every time she mentioned coming west. He left his empty sack and the fur robe at the door and joined Katie at the stove. The stove was barely large enough to hold a cooking pot or maybe two small ones, but it gave out welcome warmth.

Josh understood the stove would have been hauled up the mountain and put together at the cabin.

Katie glanced over her shoulder. "How do you know Lambert?"

The boy's face screwed up. He coughed. "Let's just say he and Pa had difficult dealings." Before Josh or Katie could comment or ask more questions, the boy pointed toward the pail of water. "Heard you was thirsty. Help yourself."

Katie drank a dipperful than handed the dipper to Josh. He drank his own dipperful.

"Thank you," he said. "Allow me to introduce us. I'm Josh Kinsley. This young lady is Katie Webster." He held out his hand to the boy.

"I'm Sam," he said, and took Josh's hand. The size of the boy's hand caused Josh to think the boy was even younger than he originally thought.

"What's a youngster like you doing out here by yourself?"

"My pa is a trapper, and I live with him. He'll be back soon." He glanced at the door. "I'm expecting him any minute now."

"Sure appreciate your hospitality." Josh glanced around. The cabin was one room that contained a narrow cot at either end. One cot had a rope suspended from one wall to the other and a blanket hung on it. Seemed one of them liked privacy. Besides the beds, there were two kitchen chairs, a small wooden table, a cupboard, an armchair made from bent willow branches, and a bookcase holding various objects, including a half dozen books. A small wardrobe stood beside the bed with the curtain beside it. "Looks comfortable," he said.

"It is." He turned to Katie. "Pleased to make your acquaintance."

She chuckled. "You didn't seem very pleased a few minutes ago."

"A person learns to be cautious."

Her mouth pursed. "I wish I'd learned that lesson sooner."

Sam stowed the gun near the stove. He'd already shoved the bar in place to prevent anyone from entering. "You're hungry?"

Katie sighed. "I've had nothing but a couple of hard biscuits and a few bites of pemmican since we made our escape." She eyed the pot on the stove from which came a savory scent that made Josh's stomach growl loudly.

Sam grinned. The boy had beautiful light blue eyes. When he got a little older, the girls would be seeking his attention. His hair was half way between blond and brown and looked to have been hacked off with a butcher knife. He wore a baggy red plaid shirt that must have been his Pa's.

"You think you might want to taste the soup I made?" He again glanced at the door. "I have it ready for when Pa comes back."

Josh could tell the boy was worried about his father.

Sam seemed to pull himself back to the cabin. "You're welcome to share it." He got two mismatched bowls from the cupboard and handed them to Josh and Katie. Darkness shrouded the room, and Sam lit a lamp and put it on the table.

Katie didn't immediately fill her bowl. "Aren't you eating?" she asked Sam.

Sam's brows furrowed. He pursed his lips. His gaze returned to the barred door. "I was waiting for Pa."

"Why not join us?" Katie's words were soft, inviting. "I'd like it. Besides, I'd feel awkward eating your food while you watched."

Sam seemed to fight a mental struggle, then he nodded and dug another bowl out of the cupboard. He set it on the table and grabbed two potholders to carry the pot to the center of the table. "Please join me." He held a chair for Katie. She smiled and thanked him.

Josh found the sudden formality amusing after the way Sam had refused to let them in. But he hid his smile and sat down as Sam drew the willow chair to the table to sit on.

"Shall we pray?" Sam could barely choke out the words. But they all bowed their heads, and he murmured the shortest prayer Josh had ever heard.

"Thanks, God."

Josh didn't dare look at Katie for fear his amusement would reveal itself.

Sam reached for Katie's bowl and filled it with the savory-smelling soup. "Rice and beans. It's a favorite of Pa's."

Katie took her bowl and inhaled the scent. "It smells delicious."

Sam filled Josh's bowl and then his own. "Dig in."

Neither Josh nor Katie needed a second invitation. Josh cleaned out his bowl in record time. "Sam, you're a good cook. It's a skill that will serve you well."

"Thanks. Pa likes good food." His eyes darted to the door.

Josh glanced at Katie. She nodded, indicating she,

too, had seen how worried Sam was. He wasn't sure what they could do. To mention it might reinforce to the boy that he had reason for worry. No doubt his father was a seasoned outdoorsman and was simply delayed.

Sam turned his attention back to the table. "I'd like to hear how you two came to be out so ill-prepared."

Revived by the nourishing food, Josh and Katie took turns relaying the story. Somehow it seemed funny now that they were safe and warm, and they laughed as they talked.

Several times, Josh found himself mesmerized by the way Katie's eyes flashed with amusement. She seemed the sort who enjoyed her life.

Lambert and Bull had done her wrong, but he guessed it wouldn't sour her on life. But perhaps it would turn her against men. Not that he could blame her for reluctance to repeat her experiences.

The truth was, when he left Ohio, it was with a vow to never again trust a young woman.

KATIE WAS SO happy to be in a warm, safe place, she was almost giddy. Even relaying the events of the past few days made her laugh. They were safe from the cold. And hopefully from Bull and his crew.

Thinking about Bull dampened her spirits. "You ever heard of this Bull? He has a mine somewhere nearby, though I can't rightly say where or how far."

"Pa did warn me to stay away from a mine that's along Beaver Creek."

"Good he warned you," Josh said. "Bull shanghais young men to do the hard work."

Sam's gaze shifted to Katie then back to Josh. "Did he expect Miss Katie to work in the mine?"

"No, he expected her to provide entertainment for him and his friends."

Sam wrinkled his brow and squinted at Katie. "What's wrong with that?"

Katie snorted. "Not the kind of entertainment that a girl wants to be part of." She knew by the way Sam's cheeks reddened that he understood. "Sorry to discon-cert you, but it isn't the sort of place or the kind of men you want to associate with."

"That's what Pa said." His voice squeaked and he cleared his throat.

Katie felt sorry for the boy, who seemed so innocent.

What Sam needed was a mother to stay with him while his pa was away and teach him about life. "Sam, where's your mother?"

"Ma died when I was ten. I've lived with Pa ever since."

"How old are you now?" Katie asked.

"How old do you think I am?" He held her gaze in a silent challenge.

Odd that he answered that way. "I don't know."

Josh broke in. "Sam, how long have you lived here with your pa?"

Sam opened his mouth to answer then realized Josh was trying to trick him. He laughed. "I'm not falling for that."

Josh chuckled. "Almost got ya."

Katie's heartstrings twanged to think of this boy

alone and so wary of strangers. Of course, he had his pa, but the man wasn't there. How often was he away, leaving young Sam to manage on his own? "Sam, it must get lonely up here."

"Mostly I have Pa for company. He'll be back soon, then you'll see what good company he is."

At the way Sam's voice cracked, Katie knew he was worried about his father.

"I hope your pa is all right." She meant her words to be encouraging, but knew they'd fallen short of that when Sam's face blanched.

"Can we pray for him?" she asked. "God has mightily answered our prayers these last two days. And even before that. I was praying to get away from Bull, and along came Josh." She grinned at him.

He grinned back. "I wasn't as prepared for the trip as I would have liked to be, but here we are, safe and sound."

Sam nodded. "A prayer wouldn't hurt nothin', I guess."

"I'll let Josh speak the words. He's much better at it than I am."

Josh opened his mouth as if to dispute the statement then clicked his teeth together and bowed his head. "Lord God, first of all, I want to thank You for guiding Katie and me to safety. Sam here is missing his pa and worried about him. He needs his pa to return. We ask You to bring him home safe and sound. Amen."

Sam looked across the room. It seemed to Katie he purposely avoided meeting either her gaze or Josh's. Poor boy was uncomfortable at having someone pray on his behalf.

Sam gave himself a shake and, rising, gathered the dishes.

"I'll help," Katie offered.

Sam chuckled, the mirth of a young boy.

Katie tried to think how old the lad was. Twelve, perhaps? Maybe younger? It was impossible to tell.

"Washing three bowls and three spoons isn't much of a chore."

Katie noted the boy used barely a cup of water to wash the dishes. She dried them and returned them to the cupboard. It held only a few dishes, some sacks, and a few other items. One sack held rice, one held beans, another held flour, and a fourth held cut oats. All were about almost full. Likely meant to last the winter. A few tins completed the inventory.

The dishes dried; she hung the towel back on the rack. She looked at Josh and grinned. His chin tipped toward his chest as if he'd fallen asleep on the hard, wooden chair.

She realized how exhausted she was and yawned.

Sam's gaze went from Katie to Josh. "Guess we should go to bed. I only got two beds. I'll sleep on the floor. Mind if I use your fur?"

Josh had wakened at the mention of bed. "Don't mind at all," he said. "But I'll be the one to use it. I have no intention of putting you out of your bed."

"I'm just a kid. I'll sleep on the floor. Besides…" His gaze went to the door. "If someone comes, you won't know if it's Pa. I will."

Katie wondered how sleeping on the floor made any difference, and from the look on Josh's face guessed he had the same thought. Josh shrugged.

"Very well. If that's the way you want it." Josh studied their surroundings. "Katie, you take the bed with the curtain."

"I need to make a trip outside first." No need to say where she meant to go. They would all be feeling the call of nature and have to trek to the outhouse.

"Here, take this." Sam lit a candle and handed it to her. She made her trip, shivering in the cold. Had the temperature dropped since their arrival? *Thank you, God, for leading us to shelter.*

Back in the cabin, she handed the candle to Josh.

"We might as well go together," Josh said to Sam.

"Nah. I'll wait until you get settled. Then I'll have one last look for Pa."

Josh studied the boy a moment, then shrugged and left the cabin with the candle in hand. He returned in a few minutes and handed it to Sam, who left.

Josh faced Katie.

"He's awfully shy," she said.

"Well, he's been with his pa since he was ten. I'm guessing he's not used to having people around apart from his pa. I can't imagine what's it's like to be so alone."

"I know what it's like. It makes a person more dependent on their parents for company. How long do you think his father has been gone?"

Josh chuckled. "Do you think he'll tell us if we ask?"

She grinned. "Try it and see. But I'd venture a guess that he will give you some indirect answer. He seems skilled at it."

Sam entered. Seeing them, he raised his eyebrows. "Thought you would have gone to bed."

"We will. Sam, tell me. How long has your pa been away?"

Sam shuffled his feet and studied the floor. "I'm sure

he'll be back tonight or tomorrow." He grabbed the fur and spread it on the floor. "I'm tired."

Katie grinned at Josh.

He shrugged, amusement dancing in his eyes.

She yawned. Her weariness returned full force. "I'm tired too. Goodnight to you both." She went to the cot assigned to her and drew the curtain across. It provided a sense of privacy, but she could hear everything. The creak of the other cot as Josh went to it. The shushing of Sam getting comfortable on the floor. The crackle of the fire.

She pulled off her boots and dress and crawled into bed.

One of the men blew out the lamp, and darkness as thick as pitch filled the room.

She tried to relax, but her nerves twitched as memories of being sold to Bull and taken to his cabin flooded her mind. The feel of his hands on her skin sent shivers up and down her spine. She pulled the quilt closer to her chin and reminded herself she was safe now. Josh had rescued her.

Josh was in the cabin. The door was barred. No one could harm her.

She fell asleep. Couldn't say for how long when a strange sound wakened her. She sat bolt upright, her heart pounding. Cold washed down her back.

5

———————

*J*osh wakened in an instant and forced himself to remain still and quiet until he could identify the sound that jerked him from his exhausted slumbers. Keening, like a woman in mourning, filled the room.

Sam? Or Katie?

He crept from the cot and tiptoed to where Sam had bedded down. The noise came from him. "Sam, are you awake?"

The keening continued, sending shivers up and down his spine.

"What is it?" Katie whispered from behind the curtain.

"Sam. He must be dreaming." He found the boy's shoulder and shook him.

Katie yawned loudly before she spoke. "Sounds more like a nightmare. Wake him up."

"I'm trying to. Sam. Sam. Wake up."

The boy gasped. The sound choked off. "What's wrong?" His voice was thin. Like a childs.

"You were dreaming."

"Oh. Sorry."

Josh wished he could see Sam, but it was too dark. He could barely make out his shape. "Are you all right? You seemed frightened."

"Or sad," Katie called. "What were you dreaming about?"

"Nothing. Can't remember. I'm all right. Go back to sleep."

Josh waited at Sam's side for a moment. The boy rolled over. Josh returned to his bed. But sleep eluded him for a long time.

Something had given Sam nightmares. Likely it was worry about his pa.

Josh vowed to do something about it, and he devised a plan during the night.

He rose the next morning at the first sound of the others stirring. "I'll get wood." He was out the door before Sam could protest. He took his time going to the shed, made a pretense of stretching and looking around as if admiring the scenery. In a way he was, but he also searched for clues. It didn't take him long to see there were no man-sized footprints around. In the woodshed, he discovered a good supply of chopped wood, which told him nothing. Sam might have chopped it, or his pa could have laid in a supply months ago, which was the more likely scenario.

In the corner of the shed stood a cupboard, and Josh went to investigate. It was a tin-lined cabinet. Solid as the finest jail cell. There were hooks in the ceiling. This was where a meat supply would be kept. But the cupboard was bare except for a skinned rabbit. So at least Sam wasn't in danger of starving.

After a few minutes, he came to a conclusion. All the evidence pointed to the fact that Sam's father had been missing a long spell.

Josh wasn't sure what to do with the information and decided to keep it to himself for a bit.

He returned to the cabin with his arms full of wood.

Katie stood at the stove. "No bacon. No eggs." Her voice had a hollow, empty ring to it. And then she brightened. "But flour to make pancakes."

Sam stood with his back to the window. Josh knew the boy had been watching him.

In short order, Katie had a stack of pancakes fried up and took them to the table. Sam brought a tin of syrup from the cupboard and again, offered a quick prayer. They ate in silence a moment.

Josh wished for a hot, strong cup of coffee, but none had been made, and he wouldn't ask for fear of making Sam uncomfortable. It could be there were no coffee beans in the house.

Katie finished first and turned her attention to Sam. "What do you do all day long...by yourself?"

The way she added the last part slowly and deliberately suggested to Josh that she meant the boy must be bored.

"I make meals for pa. Do a few chores. Gotta keep the fire going and water brought in."

"Does that take all day?" Kate persisted.

"Nope. But I got books to read." He pointed to the bookshelf along the wall.

Josh noticed a small basket by the bookshelf. "What's in there?"

Sam narrowed his eyes, as if resenting the questions. "Something of my ma's."

"Oh."

"It's some knitting she didn't finish."

"Oh." Josh glanced at Katie, hoping for some help with this conversation.

Her eyes flickered, indicating she understood. "What was she making?"

"A scarf, I guess. What does it matter?" Sam scowled at both of them.

Josh pushed back from the table. "I'll fill the water bucket." But before he even got to his feet, Sam leapt from his chair, grabbed the bucket, snagged his jacket, and shrugged into it.

"I'll do it." He was gone so fast Josh stared with his mouth hanging loose.

"The boy is surely nervous," Katie said, gathering up the used dishes and taking them to the little table that held the dishpan.

"I think he's worried. I'm going to see about finding his pa."

"That's a good idea." She leaned on the table to study him.

He could see a question building in her head. "What?"

"How long are we going to stay here?"

"It doesn't seem right to leave Sam until his pa shows up."

"Good. I feel the same." She turned back to the task of washing the dishes.

Josh went to the window to watch Sam. He'd filled

the bucket at the well but stood looking into the distance. Josh took the fur he'd used for a coat and that Sam had slept on and slung it around his shoulders.

"Nice coat," Katie said.

The innocent tone of her voice didn't fool him. She was mocking him.

It pleased him that she felt comfortable enough to do so, and he grinned. "I'm grateful for it." He chuckled. "It's an answer to prayer. I knew if I left in winter, I would need something warm. Bull never gave us coats for fear we'd run away."

Katie made a noise remarkably like a feral growl. "The man will have a lot to answer for at the end of his life." She took a slow breath. "Sure glad we got away. Tell me, how did you get the fur?"

He adjusted his boots and hat as he talked. "One night when Bull had friends over drinking, it fell off one of the horses. I saw it when I went to the outhouse and borrowed it."

She chuckled. "Are you planning to return it any time soon?"

"'Fraid not." He glanced out the window. "Here comes Sam." He waited at the door for the boy.

Sam entered. His eyes widened at the sight of Josh outfitted for the outdoors. "You're leaving?" He glanced past Josh to Katie. "Aren't you taking your friend?"

"Sam, I'm going to look for your father. Just point out where his trapline starts." He figured there'd be evidence of a trail, and he would follow it.

Sam blanched. Shook his head once. Set the bucket of water on the little worktable. For a moment, he kept his back to the room, then slowly turned. "That won't be necessary. Pa will come back when he's ready to."

"Sam, I don't mind. It's obvious you're concerned. All I mean to do is check on him. Make sure he doesn't need help."

Sam turned to stare at the bucket of water.

Josh glanced at Katie. Did she find the boy's behavior as strange as Josh did? She lifted one hand in a helpless gesture.

Sam slowly turned to face them. "Pa wouldn't want you following him."

"I feel I must. Something about this—him not returning when you expected him— isn't right." Josh reached for the door. "Your pride is getting in the way of your need for help. But if you won't tell me where the trapline starts, I'll have to find it myself." He nodded goodbye to Katie and left the house.

He had gone half a dozen steps, heading to the little shed where he'd seen evidence of a trail, when Sam burst from the cabin. "Wait. Come back. I'll tell you."

Josh retraced his steps and followed Sam inside. The boy backed away as far as the cot Josh had slept in.

"I'll tell you," he said again. And collapsed on the cot, rocking back and forth over his knees.

Josh turned a kitchen chair to face him and sat down.

Katie, her face pinched with concern, sat on the other chair.

Sam sat up, his spine straight, his face set in hard lines. "Pa's not coming back."

"What?" Katie was on her feet. "He left you here alone? You sure his name isn't Lambert?"

Sam's face twisted.

Josh murmured, "Katie, quiet."

Katie gave Josh a protesting scowl. Josh tipped his head toward Sam. One glance at his expression, and she sank back to her chair.

"I'm sorry, Sam." Her voice had softened. "Tell us what happened."

Sam shook his head. "Isn't that enough?"

Josh's mind raced. How long had the boy been alone? Could the three of them hole up here for the winter? He made up his mind.

"Do you think you could put up with us until spring, then all of us could go down the mountain?"

Sam pressed his hand to his throat. His eyes widened, and he stared at Josh. "I don't like that idea." The words seemed to exact a lot of effort from Sam.

Josh persisted. "It seems like the most reasonable solution to me. You can't stay here on your own."

Sam jolted to his feet. "Who says I can't?"

Josh understood the folly of arguing with him. "Then what do you suggest?"

Sam sank back to the cot and buried his face in his palms. "Nothing is going the way it was supposed to."

Katie went and sat beside Sam. She rubbed his back. "I know how that feels."

Josh sat on the other side of Sam. "So do I."

Katie smiled at Josh over the boy's head. "It seems to me the three of us have much in common. We can work together and make things better for all of us."

Sam shook his head. "I don't think that's possible."

"What would you like to happen?" Katie's voice was soft, beguiling, inviting Sam to confide in her.

"I'd like for my pa to be alive still." Seeming to realize

what he'd said, Sam jerked to his feet and fled to the far side of the room. He breathed hard and stared at them with wide, accusing eyes.

"He's dead?" Katie whispered.

Josh didn't speak for fear of sending Sam into further retreat.

The boy twisted his hands together then stuffed them into his trousers pockets. His teeth worried his bottom lip. At any minute, Josh feared Sam would run outside in the cold.

Katie seemed to know what to do, though, and went to Sam's side. She caught his hand and brought him back to the cot, eased him down beside Josh, and again sat on his other side. "Tell us what happened."

A shudder raced across Sam's shoulders. His voice broke as he began to speak. "He went to the mining camp. Heard there was a mule for sale. We lost ours in the spring. He made me stay here. Said he'd be back in three days at the outside." He leaned over his knees and groaned.

"It was someone else who rode in on the third day. A friend of Pa's who had stopped by a couple of times. Another trapper by the name of Chute. His horse was all lathered up. Didn't even get down. I had to grab his leg to slow him down enough for him to tell me what happened. He just said my pa was dead.

"The mule he wanted to buy belonged to Lambert Phillips. But they argued about the price. Lambert shot Pa." The boy's voice broke and grew shrill. He clamped a hand over his mouth and breathed raggedly.

Katie made shushing sounds and rubbed his back.

Josh didn't know what to do. He felt helpless in the face of the boy's loss.

Sam sucked in air like he'd forgotten he had to breathe. "I asked about Pa's stuff. Chute said he hadn't hung around to collect it. Said Phillips was out to shoot anyone who saw what he'd done. Chute said he meant to hightail it as far away as he could go. And as fast." Sam jerked up. "I asked him if he was going to tell the sheriff. Phillips should hang." The fight left Sam as quickly as it came. "Chute said there weren't no sheriff nearby. And then he was gone." The boy lowered his head to his knees and groaned.

"Sam, I'm awfully sorry." Josh squeezed the boy's slender shoulder. Sam couldn't be more than twelve, and he was all alone in the world. "When did this happen?"

Sam didn't answer. Josh met Katie's gaze. Her eyes glistened with tears.

Josh wished he could comfort both of them. His arms ached to pull Katie close and hold her as he'd done when they had sheltered together. As to Sam, the boy brought forth a protectiveness that he hadn't felt since his sisters were young.

Sam sniffed hard and sat up. "Before the snow came."

Josh did some quick figuring. If he recalled the first snow fall came— "That was three months ago." He couldn't keep the shock from his words.

Sam shrugged. "Could be."

Josh jerked to his feet. "We'll take care of you. I'll take care of both of you."

The pair looked at him. Rebellion blared from Sam's eyes. "I've been doing fine on my own."

Josh silently appealed to Katie for her support.

She scrunched her eyes up.

He knew without her saying a word that she was remembering promises made and broken, the treachery of Bull. "Katie, haven't I helped you? Gotten you to safety? Isn't it time you trusted me?"

Katie studied him, her eyes searching, exploring...

He let her delve as deep as she wanted...needed. She had to understand he was not like Lambert Phillips or Bull or even those who had bothered her back in Jefferson City.

When she finally nodded, he let out a slow, quiet breath.

"You've been honorable and good so far."

"So far." He sputtered. "Miss Katie Webster, what you've seen so far is who I am. Have you forgotten I'm a preacher's son and my sisters' favorite brother?" He did his best to sound noble.

She laughed, spoke to Sam. "He is the only brother. That's why he says that."

Sam regarded Josh with a great deal of interest.

He wondered what the boy wanted.

"Your pa is a preacher? Where?"

"Back in Verdun, Ohio. I aim to get back there just as soon as I can. I need to let them know I'm all right."

"I once knew a preacher. He took care of Ma when she died. He was nice."

"Where would that be?" Wouldn't it be something if Sam had known Pa at one time?

"Cowpatch. Little town in Kansas."

"Hmm. Never heard of it." Didn't even know if Sam told the truth or not. "That brings me back to our original conversation. I think the three of us should hole up here until spring, then trek out."

Katie nodded.

Josh waited for Sam's agreement.

Sam tossed his hands toward the ceiling. "You're going to do it even if I don't agree."

"I guess we are. Why would you object?"

Sam turned away from Josh. "Just don't suit me, is all."

Katie went to him and brushed his arm. "We'll do our best to stay out of your way. Would that help?"

The boy gave a shrill laugh and again clamped his hand to his mouth as if embarrassed at the sound that came from him." He removed his hand and waved it around the room. "Where are you going to go to be out of my way?" The accusing note in his voice scratched along Josh's nerves.

"We're here to help." Before Sam could say again that he didn't need help, Josh went on. "You'll need meat. You and I can go hunting. Katie will keep the home-fires burning, won't you?"

"I certainly will."

Sam yelled, "You don't need to take me hunting."

KATIE STARED AT SAM. She understood he was upset about his father being murdered. Someone ought to put a stop to Lambert Phillips and his foul ways. But to be so pigheaded about accepting help was simply not sensible.

Sam jammed his fists on his hips and glowered at Josh.

Josh faced the boy. Darted a glance at Katie as if asking for her help.

But she had nothing to offer. She shook her head.

"I'm a fair hand at snaring rabbits." Sam's words steamed from him. "Isn't that good enough for you?" He grabbed his coat and stormed from the house.

Josh scrubbed at the back of his neck. "The boy is certainly touchy. I don't understand it."

"Do you think he's afraid of something? You know, like Lambert. Though I can't see Lambert bothering a boy with nothing but a tiny cabin to his name."

"It doesn't make sense to me. I can't understand what's going on." Josh walked from the cot to the table. Back and forth. He ground to a halt. "A man can't even pace in this place."

Katie couldn't help it. She laughed. He had stopped inches from her, and she rubbed his arm. "Don't be a grump." She'd been longing to touch him since they'd arrived there.

The feeling alarmed her. She understood appreciating his strength while lost and cold in the snow. But they were safe now, and she didn't need it. Didn't need him. Except, they were all in this together. They had to help each other.

He grinned and caught her hand. "I'll try not to be." His smile disappeared. He rubbed at his neck. "I am concerned about Sam though. He's been alone for months. Maybe it's affected his mind."

"We'll be together for a few months. It will give us time to assess him. But it seems to me he's simply shocked. First, by the loss of his father. Then by being alone here with no way to get out. And just about the time he figures out how to manage on his own, we show up. I'd say he's had a lot to deal with for one so young."

"I think you're right. Maybe I should go see what he's up to."

"Or maybe you could let him have some space away from us."

She grinned as he again tried to pace in the tiny room. Finally, he sat on the cot.

The door flew open. Sam rushed in, grabbed a pot and a knife from the cupboard, and hurried back out.

Katie went to the window to see what he was doing.

Josh stood at her side. The narrow window necessitated they press together. She told herself she didn't have an urge to lean against him.

Josh chuckled. "Looks like he's found a way of dealing with his frustration."

Sam stood before a chopping block. Katie shuddered as he raised the knife and whacked it down. "What's he doing?"

"Cutting up a rabbit." He told her about one he'd seen hanging in the food safe.

Katie shuddered every time the knife descended. "I fear he's going to dismember himself."

Josh wrapped his arm around her shoulder and squeezed. "He seems to know what he's doing. Like he said, he's managed on his own for a while."

"I suppose there's something in that." Just as there was comfort in being held to Josh's side.

And she would not list all the reasons she shouldn't lean on him or trust him. Though, like he said, so far, he'd proven to be as solid as a rock.

Sam finished, grabbed the pot, and headed back to the cabin.

Josh dropped his arm from Katie's shoulder as the boy entered.

"Brought you rabbit for supper."

He dropped a cast-iron Dutch oven to the top of the stove. The ringing reverberated through the cabin. He tossed in some fat, dredged the pieces in flour, and browned them.

Katie and Josh leaned against the wall, watching. She, for one, enjoyed this little display of anger. It was harmless and provided some entertainment in what she thought might be a long day…a longer winter.

Josh nudged her to get her attention, and he grinned. He didn't need to say anything. She knew he was enjoying this as much as she was.

The fat spattered on Sam's hand as he turned the pieces, and he sucked the burned area. A few minutes later the meat was brown, and the room filled with the savory scent. He added water to the pot, put on the heavy lid, and faced them. His grin trumpeted his pride at proving his abilities.

"Pa said I was a good cook."

"I'd have to agree." Josh turned to Katie. "Seems we found a great place to spend the winter."

She jabbed her elbow into his ribs to warn him not to bring up their plans again, but it was too late.

Sam's scowl returned.

Determined to bring back his pleasure, she asked, "Who taught you to cook?"

"My ma. She ran a diner in…" He stopped. "Where we lived."

Katie glanced at Josh. Knew from the flash in his eyes that he had come to the same conclusion she had. Sam had made up the name of the town he reportedly came from and now couldn't remember what he'd said.

She forgot to look away from Josh. His gray-blue eyes filled with warmth. And promise? But she'd vowed to never again trust a man's promises. Strange that she couldn't remember why that was.

"The rabbit will cook all afternoon." Sam pushed the Dutch oven as far to one side as he could and retrieved the pot holding the soup from yesterday. "We'll eat this for dinner." He remained at the stove, stirring the mixture.

Katie jerked away. It was shaping up to be a trying winter, cooped up with two males. How were they going to keep from tromping on each other's toes?

She went to the bookshelf. Realizing how touchy Sam was about his space, she spoke to him. "Do you mind if I look at your books?"

He shrugged. "Guess not."

"Thanks." She examined the handful of books. They were well-worn. She'd read two of them, but four she hadn't. She hadn't realized she'd exhaled nosily, relieved to think there was something to occupy the days ahead, until Josh chuckled, close enough to her that she almost dropped the book she held.

"It's a relief to find some reading material, isn't it?" He lowered his voice. "I can tell you're worried about being stuck here with me...us...for the winter. You needn't worry. We'll manage to keep busy and keep out of each other's way."

Despite Josh's lowered voice, Sam heard. "My pa used to like to whittle."

"Good idea," Josh said, his voice overly enthusiastic, Katie decided. "What did he whittle?"

Sam laughed. The first sound of pure enjoyment Katie had heard from him. "He didn't make anything. He just whittled. The shavings went into the fire." He laughed again.

Surprised and pleased by Sam's pleasure, Katie chuckled. Josh did too. His gaze connected with Katie's and seemed to reassure her that spending the winter in the cabin could be enjoyable.

But she must not like it too much, she silently argued. This was temporary. He meant to rejoin his family in Ohio.

And she? What was she to do? She'd sold her house. Dispensed with most of her belongings. The rest had been abandoned when Lambert sold her to Bull. Bull said she wouldn't need all that stuff.

Apart from the money sewn into the lining of her coat, she had nothing left.

And nowhere to go.

It was not a comforting thought.

6

_____

The walls crowded in on Josh. How was he to spend the winter stuck in this little cabin? It reminded him far too much of the mine.

"I have to get out." He slung the fur around his shoulders and escaped into the outdoors, filling his lungs with fresh, clean air. He lifted his face to the sun and let it warm his skin. Fearing Katie would be watching from the cabin and worrying what had come over him, he strode past the little shed, and followed the trail. But the trees closed in around him, and he went back to the clearing. The opening led down the mountain, and he tromped through the snow to the edge of the hill they had climbed the day before.

He stood there, letting the brightness and openness fill his senses.

After a bit, he calmed and leaned against the nearest tree. After being in the mine or jailed in the cave, this was like a huge cathedral. His heart lifted. *God, thank You. You rescued us and brought us to safety. I vow before You to act honorably and with patience through this winter.* Songs filled his heart, and he sang softly.

He didn't know how long he remained there, but when he retraced his steps to the cabin he had been renewed. Ready to face the challenges the winter would bring their way.

The table was set when he returned. Sam and Katie seemed relieved to see him. And perhaps a little guilty.

He chuckled because he knew they had been watching out the window but didn't want him to know. "Sorry to keep you waiting."

Sam and Katie both hurried to the stove, bumped into each other, and backed away, murmuring apologies.

Josh laughed again. He couldn't help it. His heart overflowed with peace and joy.

"I'll dish up," Sam said, and brought the pot of soup to the table. They all sat. Sam filled their bowls then looked at Josh. "Seeing as you're a preacher's son, I think you should ask the blessing. If you don't mind."

"I don't mind in the least." In fact, he wanted to. He wanted Katie and Sam to know how grateful he was for everything. He bowed his head. "Father above, we want to thank You for Your many blessings. Shelter, safety, good food, and especially good friends to share it with. Amen."

He lifted his head, met Katie's gaze. Eyes as blue as the pansies Ma grew by the front steps. And as full of sweetness. A tiny smile tugged at her mouth. "Good friends, are we?"

"Indeed." His throat grew so tight at her look that he couldn't get another word out.

"Sounds nice." She ducked her head, but not before he saw how her smile widened.

Feeling particularly pleased with the world, he dug into his soup.

Sam watched them. "Friends?"

"All of us," Josh said with conviction, pleased when Sam smiled before he lowered his attention to his bowl.

Dinner didn't take long, and then the afternoon stretched ahead of them. Remembering how refreshing the trip outdoors had been for him, he waited until the little eating area was cleaned and the dishes back in the cupboard to say, "Let's all go outside and enjoy the fresh air. It's beautiful out."

Katie looked about ready to refuse than seemed to change her mind. "That could be fun."

Sam hesitated. "I've been out."

"This time is just for our enjoyment," Josh insisted.

So, the three of them donned their warm clothing and went out into the brittle sunshine. "Look how the snow sparkles. And how the tree branches are bent like the snow is white skirts. Have you ever seen a bluer sky?" He lifted his arms and face to the sky. "I will never get tired of sunshine and sky."

Katie rubbed his arm. "It's because of being kept in the dark all these months, isn't it?"

Her soft tones were a healing balm to his wounded heart.

"I hope I never have to go into a pit again in my entire life."

She leaned her head against his shoulder. "I'm glad you got free. Thank you for rescuing me. Forgive me for fighting you."

He resisted an urge to press his cheek to her head. "How were you to know who to trust?"

"Look," Sam called, pointing to the trees.

A huge white owl swooped from a branch and silently glided past them.

"Oh!" Katie watched the owl until it flew out of sight. "That was nice." She wandered away, humming quietly.

Josh's gaze followed her, glad to see her relaxing.

Sam found a branch and began sweeping the snow, creating a white cloud around him. His tongue stuck out the corner of his mouth as he focused on his task.

Josh joined Katie, nudged her to watch the boy. She grinned and whispered to Josh, "I wonder what he's thinking?"

"You think he's pretending he's sweeping us out of his cabin and off the mountain?"

She laughed.

Their gazes caught and held. Her eyes held the blue of the sky. He marveled at how seeing them gave him the same pleasure he'd had earlier in the day when he looked upward.

She sobered, chewed her bottom lip, and tipped her head as she watched him.

"What are you thinking?" he asked.

"Oh, nothing much. Just that…" She bent over and scooped up a handful of snow. "Just that Sam seems to be having fun. We should too." She tossed the snow at him. It sifted over his head, trickled under his collar, and wet his face.

He wiped his cheeks. "You want fun, do you?" He grabbed a handful of snow.

She had anticipated what he would do and backed away, but now she turned, and squealing, ran.

He had no trouble catching up to her and tossed the snow at her. Though he realized he had barely enough left in his hand to dust her coat. Bending, he scooped up more, but she raced away to the cabin. She rushed inside and slammed the door. A rasping informed him she slid the bar into place.

He peered in the window, cupping his hands to the sides of his face to see inside.

She stared at the door.

He tapped the glass to get her attention.

She grinned, enjoying her little victory.

"Katie, open the door."

She shook her head.

"You will have to sooner or later."

"I'll settle for later."

"Katie." He hoped he sounded like a man in authority.

She came to the window, pressed her hands to the glass, imitating his pose. Only the windowpane separated them. He could see a drop of water on her cheek.

He moved his finger to wipe it off, but the glass prevented it.

"Josh?" That was all. But it felt like she had offered him the whole world in that one word. Just his name.

"Are you going to open the door?" His words momentarily steamed the glass.

"Why?" The way she grinned made him want to hold her and together laugh at their troubles.

"I'm hungry," he whined.

"You just ate. Rice and bean soup. Remember?"

"That was hours ago."

"You poor dear."

"Katie, you have to understand that Bull gave us barely enough food to keep us alive and able to work. I will likely be hungry for months. Maybe years."

Her amusement fled. She turned a palm to the glass as if wanting to touch him.

He turned his palm to match hers and eased back to watch her. He felt like nothing, not even the barred door, separated them.

"Sam might run out of food." Her words were sober.

"We will survive."

She nodded. Her gaze slid past him. He turned to see what had caught her attention.

Sam stood a few feet off, watching them.

Poor Sam. He missed his parents. He was alone. So young. He needed family. But would he accept the offer of one? Or did he prefer to remain alone and independent?

When they got out of here, he would invite Sam to go with him to meet his family. He knew his parents would give Sam a home if he would accept it.

KATIE DROPPED her hands to her side and backed away from the window. What was she thinking, to be so silly?

The answer was easy. She liked Josh. Felt safe with him. After all, he had rescued her. Besides, he was a preacher's son. That ought to mean something.

Her hands curled and uncurled. Was she so needy she forgot her bitter lessons about men?

She closed her eyes as sorrow and hope mingled in a

bitter-sweet concoction. She had longed for a home of her own so badly it had made her take chances. The results had been horrible. They would have been worse without Josh rescuing her.

But her desire for home and family had not vanished.

The inside of the cabin proved too small for her troubled thoughts. She slid the bar back, opened the door, and went back outside.

Josh and Sam were in conversation. She slipped away in the opposite direction, needing time and space. Tracks she knew to be Josh's led past the woodshed, and she followed them to a trail into the woods. She continued to follow. In a hundred yards, Josh had turned back. She could see no reason to indicate why, so she continued. The peace and quiet of the woods brought calmness to her soul. The snow was only a few inches deep, but the trail climbed, and she was soon panting.

She reached a place where animal tracks abounded and stopped to study them. They appeared to be a small animal, so she wasn't concerned, and she continued onward. Recalling that Sam's father was a trapper, she kept a keen watch for any sign of a trap. A shudder shivered across her shoulders. Getting caught in one of those steel affairs would not be nice.

She broke into a clearing and gasped. The snow-draped mountains rose before her, giants against the sky. "Beautiful," she whispered. A verse her father had often quoted sprang to her mind. 'Therefore will not we fear, though the earth be removed, and though the mountains be carried into the midst of the sea—'

A thrashing sound of a heavy body coming through the trees behind her jerked her from her peace. She turned, her heart in her throat. And gasped as Josh and Sam broke into the clearing.

"You scared me." She knew her tone was accusatory, but she couldn't help it. "One minute I'm enjoying peace and quiet, and the next you barge in, making as much noise as a bear."

Josh caught her by the arms and shook her a little. "Don't wander off like that. It's dangerous."

Sam nodded. "Pa once encountered a bear up here."

"Won't they be hibernating now?" Katie looked pointedly at both of them.

The guys looked sheepish.

But Josh suddenly said, "Remember the mountain lion? They don't hibernate."

Katie was immediately contrite. "You're right. I'll be more careful in the future. But look." She caught Josh's arm as she turned back toward the mountains. "What a spectacular sight."

Josh took her hand. "It's beautiful. I've loved the mountains since I came to this area. I couldn't see them from the mine."

The way his voice deepened edged aside the peace Katie had enjoyed a moment ago. It pained her to think of what Josh had endured.

"My father used to quote a verse from the Bible. 'Though the mountains be shaken, and the hills be removed, yet my unfailing love for you will not be shaken.'"

Josh relaxed. "I know that passage. It's from Isaiah."

"It's strange. I'd forgotten how Father used to quote that. He was a quiet but firm man. I remember one time a man wanted Father to help with a deal that Father considered less than honest. He said cutting the corners as he'd been asked to do was legally acceptable. But he said it wasn't morally right, and that mattered more to him. Mother told me it had cost him a large business deal, but she agreed with his decision."

Josh leaned his shoulder against hers. As if they shared something special in the moment. He didn't speak. He didn't need to. His presence was enough.

Sam wandered around the clearing, kicking at the snow as if he searched for something.

Josh watched him a moment. "Are you looking for something?"

Sam didn't answer, just continued to stomp and attack the snow.

Katie turned to face Josh. "Is he all right?" she whispered.

"I don't know."

They watched a few more minutes.

"Something is wrong." Katie went to Sam and caught his arm. "Sam, what's the matter?" She looked closer at him. "You're crying."

"No. I'm not." He swiped at his tears and stomped away.

Katie silently appealed to Josh. Did he understand this?

He shook his head. He watched Sam for a moment then went to the boy, caught him by the shoulder. "Sam, if you're looking for something, we can help. Just tell us what it is you're seeking."

"Nothin'." Sam's voice broke, and he ran to the side of the clearing.

Katie hurried to him. "Oh, Sam. Let us help you."

"You can't help," he shouted. "You can't take back the bad things I said to Pa last time we came here. To this very spot." He stomped his foot. "I asked Pa if I could have a dog." He glowered at Katie and then Josh. "A person gets lonely up here, you know."

Katie nodded and pressed her hand to his arm. "I know."

"Pa said a dog was nothin' but trouble. I got mad and said things I shouldn't have. And now he's gone, and I can't say I didn't mean them." The words ended on a wail.

Katie reached her arms out, meaning to hug Sam. He jerked away. "Don't touch me."

"I'm sorry. I just want to let you know I care."

"Don't care." He stomped away.

"I'm sure your pa understood. We all say things we don't mean."

"Leave me alone."

She wanted to point out he might be saying things right now that he would regret later.

Josh pulled her close, holding her to his side. "He's hurting."

"I know."

Sam went to the edge of the clearing where the trees closed in. He fell to his knees. His shoulders shook.

Katie pressed her lips together and blinked as she watched the boy suffering alone.

Josh tightened his hold on her. "Leave him be. It's something he has to deal with on his own."

"I hate not being able to do anything."

"I know. So do I." He took her hand and led her back to the path.

She stopped a few yards into the trees, unable to

continue, as her heart bled for Sam. "I know the need to mourn and wish someone would journey with you. When Father died, I had my mother, but she was already suffering from pain and weakness. I felt I had to be strong for her. Then when she died, my friends were all married and moved on. Most of them came to the funeral and expressed their condolences, but then I was all alone. Maybe that's why I was so eager to marry." Tears were streaming down her face, but she could no more stop them than she could make it suddenly become spring.

Josh pulled her into his arms, pressing her face to the hollow of his shoulder. "I'm here now. I'll hold you while you cry."

And she did just that. The tears poured out like a dam had broken. Her sobs were quiet, coming from a deep well of sorrow she had never before allowed expression.

After a bit, she quieted, but did not want to leave the shelter of his arms.

He rubbed her back and held her.

She remembered Sam. Alone. Sorrowing without the comfort of others. She straightened and glanced back along the path. "I don't like to leave him. We should wait here for him."

"He knows the way back. Let's go to the cabin. If he doesn't return soon, I'll go after him."

"Very well." His suggestion made sense, so they made their way back to the yard. The path was narrow, or she would have clung to his hand.

They returned to the cabin. How alone they were. For months, they would only have each other for company.

The idea should have frightened her but instead, it comforted her.

Josh put another log in the stove.

Katie checked the stewing rabbit. It smelled wonderful. They would need something more than that to eat though, so she set rice to cook. Still Sam hadn't returned, and she joined Josh at the window to watch for him.

After a bit, Josh turned away. "Let's sit at the table. Pretend we're not worried. Then when he comes in, he won't be quite so embarrassed."

She took one more look and then sat across from him. "I can't imagine how he's managed this well. He's just a boy. But to think of him alone here for the winter…." She shuddered. "Maybe God led us here for Sam's sake as well as ours."

"I'm sure that's so."

The door rattled. He was back, and Katie could finally breathe easier.

Sam rushed in, left the door open as he dashed to the small wardrobe cupboard at the end of the cot where Katie had slept. He threw open the door, rustled around inside, slammed the door shut, and rushed back outside. Thankfully, he closed the door behind him.

She let out a gust of air. "What was that about?"

The door of the wardrobe swayed open.

She stared at the contents inside. It didn't make sense.

"Josh." She stepped back so he could see inside the wardrobe. "What do you see?"

7

*J*osh stared after Sam. What was the boy up to? Then at Katie's surprised words, he shifted his attention to the wardrobe. A coat, a red shirt, and some trousers were hooked to nails. Nothing he didn't expect to see. But hung on the other side was a girl's dress.

"What would they be doing with a dress?"

He followed Katie to the wardrobe. She lifted the fabric of the dress. Dark blue with sprigs of flowers scattered across the skirt. She let the dress fall back and picked up something from the shelf. "Hair ribbons. They've been used."

Josh could see where knots had been tied. In fact, a blue ribbon still had a bow in it.

"These are a young girl's things." Katie sounded as confused as Josh felt.

She put the ribbons back. "I don't understand."

They faced each other.

Josh tried to make sense of the discovery. "Did Sam have a sister?"

"She's not here. Where is she?" Katie's eyes widened. "Did she die?" She pressed her hand to her mouth. "If so… Poor Sam. What are we going to do?"

Josh eased Katie to his side and firmly secured the wardrobe door. "What can we do? I don't believe he meant for us to see this. We snooped, but that doesn't give us the right to probe into his life."

"But the poor boy." She clung to Josh's arm and buried her face against his shoulder as if she couldn't bear the idea of Sam enduring more pain. "He doesn't need to carry his sorrow alone." Her voice was muffled.

Josh cupped his hand over her head. It pained him to see her so troubled just as much as it hurt to think of all that Sam had endured. "At least we are here to help him through the winter. Come spring, we'll take him down the mountain with us."

She leaned back so she could see his face. "Then what will become of him?"

"I've considered taking him to my parents. They'd gladly give him a home. But the idea doesn't seem quite right for a boy raised as he's been. He's used to living like this."

"Are you planning to stay in Ohio with your family?"

"I don't think so. I like this country. I think after I see them, I'll come back and start over."

"Gold mining?"

He shuddered. "Never. I'll find something that lets me see the sky and feel the sun on my face." He'd never return to panning for gold either. He wanted something more certain. "I think I'd like to take up ranching. I tried that work before the allure of gold distracted me. I enjoyed it."

She smiled as if the idea had her approval. "You could keep him with you."

"Me? I'm not married. I don't have a home."

"Didn't you just say you were going to start over? All you need to do is include him in your plans."

"I like that. If he agrees, I'll make it work."

She patted his shoulder. "Oh, he will. You have all winter. That's more than enough time for him to grow fond of you."

"That's all it takes?" He meant to sound teasing, but knew it sounded like he wanted her approval. Which he did.

"I don't think it will take long." Her gaze was steady and full of promise.

Sam entered the cabin and studied them with narrowed eyes. Daring them to mention the tears they'd seen up the hill. His gaze darted to the wardrobe. The door had remained closed. "What are you doing?" Challenge rang from his words.

"Discussing the future," Josh said before Katie could blurt out anything else. He guided her back to the table. "If we're to leave here in the spring, we need to start making plans." There was plenty of time, but they all needed a project...something to occupy themselves. "Sam, sit down and help us."

With about as much enthusiasm as a man led to the gallows, Sam sat at the end of the table.

Both he and Katie regarded Josh, waiting for him to speak. It wasn't like he'd given this a whole lot of thought, so it took him a moment to come up with something. "Sam, would you know the closest town?"

Sam blinked as if the question surprised him. "I suppose that would be Glory. There was a nice preacher man there last time we went."

"In my experience preacher men are nice."

"You say that because your father was nice," Katie sounded wistful.

"Yes, I do." He turned back to Sam. "Is Glory the name of a town?"

Sam chuckled. "Yup."

"Is it in Montana Territory?"

"Yup."

That was good news. "How far is it to this town?"

Sam leaned back in his chair. "It took us four days to come from there. And that was with Old Mulie carrying our supplies."

It would go downhill for them. "So, we need to plan on four days. Five, maybe. Do you think you remember the way?"

"Sure." The words were spoken with lots of confidence. Then Sam shrugged. "I think so. Pa always pointed out landmarks when we traveled. Told me to always pay heed to where I was going."

"I'm sure you'll do just fine." If they got anywhere near a town, they would encounter ranch homes or settlers. Or at the very least, a trail or even a road. "This time I'd like to be properly prepared for the trip. That means a supply of food that is easy to carry on our backs."

Sam and Katie waited for him to continue.

"I'd say we should have dried meat and biscuits at the very least."

"Pa used to make rice and bean patties to carry with him." Sam was suddenly animated. "I could make some of those and let them freeze in the larder." His face drew into flat plains. "Except I'm not going. This is my home."

Katie reached out to take Sam's hand, but the boy jerked back.

Katie withdrew. She bit her bottom lip.

Josh knew she was stung by the boy's continued rejection of her offers of comfort. He wished he could ease her hurt. "You're welcome to come. But even so, perhaps you'll help us get ready."

"Gladly."

In Josh's mind, Sam was far too eager to see them gone, especially for one so young and alone. But they would be together all winter. It would give Josh plenty of time to convince Sam he should leave this place.

Sam and Katie went to get the food that simmered on the stove. As they ate the nutty rice and tasty rabbit, they discussed what they could do to prepare for the spring trip.

Besides preparing the food they would need, they agreed they would need a way to carry their supplies. The project gave them something to work together on.

They sat around the table, enjoying the simple meal and made plans.

"I'll go with you to trap rabbits tomorrow," Josh said. "We can start drying meat."

Sam appeared anything but pleased as he gave a reluctant, "Fine."

The meal was cleaned up, and the evening stretched

out before them. They could go to bed, but it was too early despite it being dark outside.

"I have an idea," Josh said. "Sam, do you know how to play checkers?"

"Maybe."

Josh's gaze went across the table. "Katie?"

"I understand the concept."

"Sam, would you have any objection to me drawing out the game board on the table?"

The boy shrugged.

"Do you have a pencil?"

Sam brought one from the bookshelf.

Josh drew out the squares, shading in every second one to create a checkerboard. He cast about for something to use for game pieces. He saw nothing inside, but he knew just the thing. He lit a candle. "I'll be back in a moment." At the woodshed, he dug through the shavings and chips until he found two dozen round pieces of approximately the same size. They would do. He blackened half with charcoal.

He returned to the house and set out the game. He explained how it was played to Sam, who sat across from him.

The first game went quickly, as Sam was only learning and made it easy for Josh to win. They played several games, with Sam improving on each one.

"I almost won that time," he chortled.

"You caught on real fast."

Each game took longer as Sam carefully considered his moves.

Josh used the time to study Katie. She watched the game. No doubt learning a few skills.

She turned, saw he watched her, and a smile filled her eyes.

Their gazes went on and on, searching and exploring.

She put her hand to her heart. It was a gesture of vulnerability that filled Josh with fierce protectiveness. He felt responsible for her in a way that defied reason. He could only explain it as a feeling that developed as they fought the elements while wandering in the snow.

He wanted to hold her and assure her they were safe. He would make sure they were throughout the winter with its challenges of surviving high in the mountains. He would protect her even though Bull might still be trying to track them. "When we get out," he said, half to himself, "I'm going to let the sheriff know about Bull's mining operation."

"Will you tell him about Lambert Phillips murdering my pa?" Sam's voice grated with anger.

"I surely will." Though, unless there were individuals who had witnessed the murder and were willing to testify, there would be little the sheriff could do.

Josh turned his attention back to the game, but he'd lost enjoyment in it. He must stay on guard and alert against every kind of danger—especially Bull.

They went to bed shortly after that, but Josh could not sleep. *Lord, please keep us safe.*

He had almost dozed off when something rattled on the roof. A low growl. Was a mountain lion stalking them?

THE NEXT MORNING he made sure to be the first one out of the cabin and had a good look around. But half an hour of scouring the yard and the surrounding area yielded no sign of tracks from a big cat. Had he dreamed it? He must have. Or perhaps he had been dreaming of the mountain lion that had threatened them as they escaped Bull. Either way, he was relieved to know there was no imminent danger.

Over breakfast, he announced his intention of going after rabbits. "I could use your expertise," he said to Sam.

The way Katie smiled at him for how he broached the subject made Josh feel ten feet tall.

Sam reluctantly agreed, and they set out as soon as the meal was over. Katie escorted them to the door. She squeezed Josh's arm. "You two have a good time. I'm going to make biscuits as my contribution."

Basking in her approval, Josh let Sam lead the way down the slope to a treed area. Josh made out tracks from rabbits. Sam showed him how he set up a snare.

"I'm impressed," Josh said. "You really know what you're doing."

Sam snorted. "I'll leave you here and go yonder to set up snares there."

Josh nodded although Sam didn't need to make it so obvious that he couldn't wait to escape his company. Following Sam's directions, Josh packed a little trail to attract the rabbits and set up a snare. He did this several times. Each time, according to Sam's instructions, he marked the place with a bit of rag so he could find the snare the next day.

Satisfied with the morning's work, he went in search of Sam. He followed Sam's tracks into the trees and stopped to listen. Hearing the boy moving, he went toward the sound.

A flicker ahead caught his attention. Sam. With his trousers down, going to the bathroom.

Josh took a step closer then stopped. The boy would want his privacy.

The boy was half hidden behind the bushes, but Josh saw enough to know he was squatting then he saw steam. It took a full minute for Josh to realize what he was witnessing.

Sam was no boy. He was a girl.

He couldn't decide what to do. Should he confront Sam or back away and pretend he didn't know? Backing away seemed the better choice, and he retreated a step. His foot landed on a twig. It cracked, the noise like thunder in the stillness.

Sam jerked his trousers up and spun around. His—*her* mouth fell open and then snapped shut, and the glower she gave Josh was enough to melt the snow for twenty paces.

Josh waved. "Found you. I got four snares set. How many did you do?" *Bluff. Bluff. Don't let him know you saw him.* Her.

Eyes narrowed to slits, Sam studied Josh.

"Are you ready to go back?" Josh asked. "It must be close to dinnertime." He made a show of studying the sky as if trying to judge the time of day. Did Sam realize Josh had seen her?

At a loss to know how to deal with the situation, he said nothing as Sam joined him and they began the return journey. They were halfway back when Sam stopped.

"What did you see?"

"Lots of rabbit tracks. Maybe tracks of a big cat too. Katie and I heard one when we were out in the snow."

Sam curled his hands into fists and glowered at Josh. "That's not what I'm talking about."

With no idea of what to say, Josh shrugged. "You'll have to help me out."

He met Sam's eyes, forcing himself not to blink, not to reveal anything in his gaze. Nothing but innocence and curiosity.

Sam stomped away two feet then ground to a halt and again faced Josh. "I know you seen me."

Josh nodded. "Uh huh." Let the boy...correction, girl...decide what that meant.

"Whatcha gonna do about it?" The girl played a good game of bluff.

"What should I do?" Josh had more years bluffing than a half-grown kid. And it had been honed to perfection working in Bull's mine.

Sam turned, arms crossed her over chest as she stared away from Josh. Slowly, the fight left her...

Josh wasn't sure what to call Sam. It'd mostly be up to Sam whether or not she wanted to continue this pretense.

"Are you going to tell Katie?" The words were soft, pleading, as if Sam was afraid.

Josh went to Sam's side, careful not to touch her. "Sam, it's time for you to be clear what you're talking about."

Sam turned, her mouth pursed, eyes flashing. "You seen me having a leak, didn't you?"

"And if I did?"

"Then you know."

Josh would not be the first to bring the truth out. He figured that was up to Sam. "Know what?" Seeing Sam's frustration mounting, he added, "Sam, you have to be brave enough to come right out and say what you're talking about. Pretending and skirting the issue won't rectify it."

"Rectify? What's that mean?"

Josh had to consider a moment how to explain it to her. "Won't make it right."

Sam stared at Josh. She breathed hard.

Josh didn't care to see the youngster struggling. "Come on. Let's get back before Katie starts to worry." He stayed at Sam's side, silent. He was certain Katie would understand and be supportive of the predicament Sam faced.

They reached the yard. Sam had not spoken since they had resumed their return journey.

If she meant to keep the truth about who...what she was, what was Josh to do?

Should he tell Katie or keep it a secret out of respect for Sam's decision? The idea of keeping the truth from Katie did not sit well with him.

As soon as Sam and Josh entered the cabin, Katie sensed the tension between them. She glanced from one to the other. Sam avoided her gaze. Josh's smile was half-hearted.

She was about to ask what had happened when Josh gave a little shake of his head. Understanding that he had signaled her to not ask questions, she nodded and went to the stove. "I spent the morning baking biscuits." It was a challenge with no oven, but as she made her way west on the train, she'd overheard a wizened old cowboy bragging to the man beside him that he made the best biscuits you could ever hope to taste. "And in a Dutch oven over a fire." The statement had caught her attention. She had tried it and was pleased with the result. But it was slow going, as she could only do eight at a time.

There was leftover rabbit and rice for dinner and fresh biscuits. She set the food out. Sam and Josh sat at the table. Josh asked the blessing, and they dug in.

Katie had spent the morning alone and was anxious for talk even if the other two seemed to have taken a vow of silence. "I am finding the little stove handy to cook on."

Josh grunted. He seemed consumed with downing biscuits as fast as he could.

He had warned her that he would likely be hungry for a long time.

They finished up the rice and rabbit. Sam rose and got the syrup pail. He and Josh continued to eat biscuits, now drowned in syrup.

"Do I let the biscuits dry out or freeze whatever is left after our meal?" The hope of having any left was rapidly vanishing.

"They'll not spoil if they're dried out," Josh mumbled around a mouthful of biscuit.

"They're softer if they aren't dried out," Sam mumbled. The first words he'd spoken since he and Josh returned to the cabin.

"Do you both like the biscuits?"

Josh swallowed hard and stared at her. "They're excellent."

"Yup." Sam said.

Katie grinned, feeling like she'd won a great prize.

The pair finally slowed down. Josh leaned back in his chair. Sam sat forward.

Katie's gaze went from one to the other. "Is someone going to tell me what's going on?"

Josh tipped his head toward Sam, which earned him a fierce scowl.

"Sam?" Katie's voice was soft, begging. "Is something wrong?"

Sam jerked to his feet so fast the willow chair skidded back to the cot. He planted his fists on the table and leaned forward. "I'm a girl." He practically snarled at Josh. "Are you satisfied?" He grabbed his coat and fled outdoors.

Katie stared after him, jumping when the door slammed. Slowly, in disbelief, she brought her gaze to Josh. "What did he say?" Surely, she had misunderstood.

"She told you she is a girl."

"A girl." It still wasn't making sense.

Josh told about discovering Sam relieving herself. "I had decided not to say anything, but she guessed I'd seen. But she didn't admit it until now."

"Sam's a she? That would explain the dress in the wardrobe. But why pretend otherwise?"

"I expect her pa thought it would make it safer for her."

Thinking of men like Lambert Phillips and Bull and Bull's friends, Katie shuddered. "He was probably right."

Josh reached across the table and cupped his hand over hers. "Not all men are like that."

A smile came from a tender, sweet spot in her heart. "I know." She knew he wasn't. "What are we to do now?"

Josh squeezed her hand. "I think it's up to Sam." He shifted so he could see the door. "I'll give her a bit of time to think this through, then if she doesn't come back, I'll go find her."

"*We'll* go find her."

Josh nodded. "We are all in this together, and she needs to understand we only want to help her."

While they waited, Katie tidied up the cooking area. She washed the few dishes, and Josh dried them.

"Let's go find her," Josh said when they'd finished.

At that moment, the door banged open, and Sam came in. She closed the door and stood with her back to it, her gaze on the floor. "You might as well hear it all."

Katie's throat clamped off at the defeated note in Sam's voice. All sorts of frightening scenarios raced through her mind. Maybe the man who had brought her here wasn't really her pa. Maybe he'd used her poorly. Katie forced herself to stop thinking along those lines. No need to judge the now-dead man as being like Phillips or Bull.

She sucked in a deep breath and prepared to hear Sam's story calmly.

8

"My name is Samantha Rimmer. I think my pa named me that because he wanted a boy. Calling me Sam was the only way he could get what he wanted."

Katie longed to leap up and ask if that's why he'd had Sam pose as a boy. Josh must have sensed her thoughts, for he reached for her hand and squeezed it. She turned her palm toward his and clung to his strength.

Sam continued in a monotone. "My ma died when I was ten, and I came to live here with Pa. Before that he would visit us. We lived in Independence, Missouri." She flashed them a look brimming with a so-there challenge then returned to studying the floor. "At first, I wore dresses. Pa seemed to like it, but by the time I turned twelve—almost a year ago—I was no longer a little girl." Her cheeks flared red enough that Katie could see them even though Sam kept her head down. "That's when he said I ought to dress like a boy. He told me to keep my hair short and wear baggy clothes." She sighed. "Sure hated seeing my hair go.

"He taught me how to survive in the bush. I think he was afraid something would happen to him. More than once he told me never to trust anyone, and never let them know I was a girl."

Her head came up. Her gaze brimmed with pleading. "I had to lie. Don't you see?"

Katie went to her side and took Sam's hands. She expected the girl to pull away as she had at every previous effort to touch her, but Sam seemed to welcome the gesture.

"I understand why you did it. I would have done the same thing if I was in your situation." Katie studied Sam's face then gave a little chuckle. "I have to say, I always thought you were too pretty to be a boy."

Sam's cheeks burned red. "Truly?"

Josh took the two steps necessary to join them. He put one arm around Katie's shoulder. "I thought the same." He raised his other arm to put around Sam's shoulders, but at the way Sam sucked in her cheeks as if holding her breath and waiting for danger to pass, he lowered his arm and tightened his hold on Katie.

Katie understood Josh longed to comfort Sam. But he'd have all winter to teach the girl to trust a man. There was no time like the present to begin that journey. "Some men can be trusted," she murmured.

Josh chuckled. "Thank you."

Sam's gaze went to Josh and then back to Katie. Her face screwed up. "What now?"

Katie turned to Josh, waiting for him to give his opinion.

"I think"—he spoke slowly as if forming his words as he spoke—"your pa was right. I know Katie and I are the only ones here right now, but you can never tell when someone might happen by."

Katie jerked her attention to the door. Did he think Bull was still on their trail? She looked at the gun. It might be a good idea to learn to use it.

Josh continued. "While we're here it's best if you appear to be a boy."

Sam nodded. "Pa would say the same." She broke away hurriedly.

Katie knew it was a lot for the girl to absorb. Having hidden as a boy for so long, she likely feared having the truth about her revealed. Having been taught to mistrust others she would find it hard to trust. Katie wanted to reassure her. "Both Josh and I will make sure you are all right."

Sam sat on the edge of the bed, his hands hanging down between his legs...her legs.

Katie would need some time to get used to thinking of Sam as a girl.

Josh squeezed Katie's shoulders, and she lifted her gaze to his face. He'd guided her across the snow-covered landscape, sheltered her in the cold, and now shared the cabin with her and Sam, making her feel safe. She was learning to trust him. Sam would too.

"I'd like to see those mountains again," Josh said. "Who would like to go with me?"

Katie said she would, but neither she nor Josh moved toward the door as they waited for Sam's decision.

She pushed wearily to her feet, grabbed her coat, and went out the door.

Josh and Katie followed, letting her go ahead. They both seemed to have the same idea, that Sam needed time alone to sort things out.

Whereas being alone was the last thing Katie wanted. She chuckled softly.

"What's so funny?" Josh said.

She explained, adding, "I've had quite enough of being alone and lonely."

He chuckled. "Strange as it seems, seeing as I was barely allowed any privacy at the mine, I share the feeling. Those men were not good company."

"Not like me, you mean?" She pretended to preen.

He laughed outright, startling birds from the trees in a noisy rush. "Not the least bit like you." He caught her hand and pulled her into a run up the hill.

Sam stood to one side, her face toward the mountain view.

Josh led Katie to the top of the hill where the view was the best. He kept hold of her hand as they stopped to gaze at the beauty. He sighed. "I could never get tired of seeing the mountains."

Katie's heart filled with joy and peace, due only in part to the scene. For the next few months the three of them would be together, shut away from the rest of the world. Worries and fears belonged in that far-off place. They did not exist here.

JOSH COULD HAVE STAYED in the clearing, admiring the mountains, until dark. With Katie at his side, holding his hand, and Sam leaning on a nearby tree, her expression soft as she remained lost in her thoughts, he couldn't think of any place he'd sooner be or anything he'd sooner do.

Neither Katie nor Sam seemed inclined to return to the cabin.

Katie sighed. "I haven't felt this peaceful since before my father passed on." She leaned her head against Josh's shoulder. "Isn't it a shame that the whole world can't enjoy this every day?"

"It would get a little crowded on this hill, don't you think?" he teased her.

She chuckled. "I mean to carry the feeling here wherever I go." She pressed her hand to her chest.

"That's a nice idea. There've been times in the past I could have used this peace." He smiled at her. Would she guess he meant the sense of rightness he felt at her side every bit as much as he meant the joy of regarding the mountains?

"Like when you were in the mine?" She turned toward him; her expression sober. "I'm so glad you were there when I needed help, but I wish, for your sake, you hadn't been."

He understood what she meant. "Thanks. But for your sake, I'm glad I was."

She studied his face as if memorizing every single crease and whisker. A smile began at her eyes and filled them with sparkles to rival that of the snow around them. Then she grinned. "Just think, if something hadn't driven you to go west, you might never have seen the mountains."

"I surely wouldn't have wanted to miss this view." He wasn't looking at the scenery, but at Katie.

Her cheeks blossomed a very becoming pink.

She lowered her gaze. "If I recall correctly, you once hinted that something happened that made you leave your family and come west. Care to tell me what it was?"

It no longer bothered him to think of Eliza. He didn't mind telling Katie about her. "When I graduated from college, I accepted a job as clerk in a prestigious law firm. You won't care what the name is. The senior partner had a pretty eighteen-year-old daughter who came frequently to the office and was friendly and flirtatious with me."

"Wait. What was her name?"

"Eliza."

"Oh, nice name." Katie's voice was very small.

Josh chuckled. "Unfortunately, it didn't translate into the girl's behavior. I was encouraged by her attention and began to court her. We always went to the events she wanted to attend. I fancied myself in love with her. In hindsight, I think I was flattered by the attention."

"Really? That doesn't sound like you."

Katie's words made him happy all over. "I was young and foolish." He felt he'd aged decades in the intervening two years. "Anyway, I soon learned how she viewed me. One day she came into the office clinging to the arm of the junior partner in the firm. A man twenty years her senior. She smiled at me and leaned over to whisper that she was grateful for my help in getting the man's attention. I was hurt and angry to realize she'd been using me without telling me and said so. She informed me my future lacked promise...whatever she meant by that. I later realized she wanted someone with lots of money. I admit I was blinded by her looks and her ways. Anyway, I couldn't stay there. That's when I decided to head west. I reasoned a change of scenery and a little adventure would cure me of my broken heart."

Katie wrapped her arms around Josh's waist. "I hope your broken heart is healed."

He held her close, his cheek to her head. "It is now." Let her think he meant the trip west had done its work but holding her in his arms had the power to heal any hurt.

"Are you two going to get all mushy?" Sam made her disgust clear.

Josh released Katie, and they both laughed.

Josh gazed another minute at the scene before him, knowing he would never forget either the mountains or the time shared with Katie, and then they made their way down to the cabin.

OVER THE NEXT few days they all kept busy preparing food for the spring trip. Josh and Sam skinned the rabbits and hung strips of meat in the cabin to dry. It was a slow process, but as the days passed, the store of dried meat in the food cupboard grew.

Meanwhile, Katie baked biscuits. She bemoaned the fact that so few of them made it to their stash of food.

"It's your fault for making them taste so good," he teased.

Sam and Katie worked together creating the rice and bean patties, which they allowed to freeze and added to the supply in the food cupboard.

In the evenings, they played checkers. Both Sam and

Katie had become challenging adversaries. Unfortunately for the peace and quiet in the cabin, they both gloated loudly whenever they won.

Josh always laughed because he didn't care if he won or lost. He simply enjoyed Katie's company. But one day he took stock. At this rate they would soon have all the food they would need for the trip, and then how would they pass the long winter?

"We need to get outside more," he said.

Both Sam and Katie looked at him like he'd announced he meant to go swimming in the snow.

He laughed. "We need to have some fun and get out of this room, or we'll end up with cabin fever."

Sam and Katie regarded each other. Sam shrugged and rolled her eyes.

Katie grinned at the girl then asked, "What is cabin fever?"

Josh gave a fake shudder. "After a time of being closed in such a tiny room"—he waved his arm around to indicate what he meant—"people begin to feel cooped up. Often they turn on their companions." He shuddered again. "I've heard of people doing awful things to each other when they snap."

Katie and Sam grinned at each other, and they both nodded.

What was going through their minds? He didn't have to wait long to find out. They jumped toward him, one on either side, and held out their hands like claws.

"Like this?" Katie growled, and she and Sam dug their talons into his ribs.

He laughed. He squirmed. He tried to shove them

away, all to no avail. Then he squeezed them both in a bear hug, making it impossible for them to move.

They giggled.

He pressed a kiss to the top of each head, and Katie lifted her face to him, full of happiness and trust.

It was the first time Sam had allowed him to touch her, and his heart swelled with affection for the girl.

She broke away, grabbed her coat. "Let's go outside."

Josh and Katie followed her up the hill to the scene they all enjoyed.

Neither Katie nor Josh spoke as they watched Sam. What would she do next? She squatted on the brow of the hill, her eyes on the mountains. Josh and Katie stood on either side. Katie rested her hand on Sam's shoulder.

Fearful his touch would offend the girl, Josh placed a tentative hand on her other shoulder. When she didn't bolt or object, he squeezed lightly.

"You should see this place in the summer." Sam's words were soft as if she spoke to herself. "Wildflowers like a pretty carpet. I always wished Ma had been able to see it. When I told Pa that, he said she had never wanted to venture so far from her home. I think she was afraid of change. Too bad she never set aside her fears."

Josh and Katie glanced at each other. Did she think the same as he...that Sam would have to face her fears if she was to leave the cabin? But he didn't voice his opinion. Sam had time to come to her own conclusions, and he couldn't see she would choose anything but to go with them.

Sam seemed eager to talk, and he didn't mind listening.

"Ma liked living in Independence. Like I said, she ran

a diner. That's where she met Pa. I don't think she meant to fall in love with him. He worked as a wheelwright. Business was good but Pa wasn't content. Ma said he couldn't bear to watch all the wagons going west and not be on his way. One day he announced he was going. He said he would look around and come back for Ma. I was born that winter. Pa came back but never to stay." She sighed. "I never truly had both parents at the same time."

She shifted to regard Katie and then Josh, a smile teasing her lips. "I remember telling Ma that I really needed grandparents and asked her where they were. She said they were all gone. When I came here, I asked Pa the same thing. He said his parents had both died when he was young." She slumped over her knees. "Now I don't even have parents."

"I have an idea," Josh said. "You can be part of my family."

"I don't know."

Hoping to make her see how life could offer her what she wanted, Josh told more about his adopted sisters. She seemed interested, but he didn't push the idea.

Near as he could figure it was early December, so they had all winter.

Over the next few days, they continued to prepare for the trip out. Josh made sacks they could carry on their backs. They made a daily journey outside, usually to the hilltop, to gaze at the mountains. And they talked. Katie told stories about her family. Sam told how her pa had taught her so many things, but both gals liked to hear about Josh's sisters. He had a store of memories to share with them.

He finished the sacks and showed them to Katie and Sam.

"I have an idea," Katie said. "Let's put a few things in them and wear them up the hill. Make sure they aren't uncomfortable."

Josh allowed that it was a good idea. "What do you want to carry?" It was just practice, so it didn't matter.

"I don't know." Katie grabbed a quilt off her cot and folded it into the sack. "Maybe a pot or two so we can see how the weight will be." She chose a pot and a frypan.

Sam stuffed two books in hers and looked around for something more. "I'll take the quilt from your bed," she said to Josh.

They hooked the sacks over their shoulders and adjusted them until they were satisfied then both of them turned to Josh.

"What?" he said, pretending not to know what they wanted.

"Put something in yours," Sam said.

"Okay." He wrapped the latest batch of biscuits in a tea towel and put them in. "There we go."

Katie shook her head. "Do you think you will ever get over being hungry?"

"I might. About the time I lose all my teeth and am reduced to gumming my food." He sucked in his lips and smacked like a toothless old man.

"So next year?" Sam seemed so innocent and sincere that Josh began to explain what he meant, which reduced her to gales of laughter.

Katie chuckled. "She got you."

Josh grabbed their hands and dragged them out the door and across the yard. They escaped and ran ahead of him. Sam paused to call, "Are you slowing down already?"

He charged after them. By the time he caught up to them a hundred yards later, they were all reduced to wheezing laughter.

The trail was too narrow to go three abreast. Sam went ahead, and Josh and Katie followed more slowly, walking side by side although it crowded them together.

"It's good to see Sam relaxing around us," Josh said.

"She's a bright young girl. Her parents taught her well. She showed me how to make those rice and bean cakes."

"Like she said, her pa worried she would have to manage on her own. It's a testament to his teaching that she's done so well."

"How long do you think she could have managed on her own?"

Josh considered it a moment. "There are supplies enough to last until spring. Her father would have planned to trek out then and take his furs to market. I don't know what she would have done."

"She would have figured it out. She knows the way to Glory. I think she would have gone there."

"I think God sent us to help her."

Katie smiled. "I think so too."

They followed Sam to the crest of the hill, and they all sighed at the sight. The sun hung over the mountains, sending golden fingers into the draws.

After a few minutes of admiring the scene, Josh asked if the sacks had been comfortable.

"Tolerable," Katie said. "I think I could carry mine down the mountain." She shifted it off her shoulders and dropped it to the ground beside her. Sam followed her example. They both sat on the ground where it was worn down to grass from their frequent visits.

"I wonder how Toad is doing." Josh worried Bull might take out his anger on the man.

"Toad?" Katie and Sam said in unison.

Josh sat beside them. "Toad was one of the guards at the mine. The nicest one of them."

"Is Toad his name?" Sam asked.

"It's the only name we knew. I don't know who first called him that, but it was obvious why they had. If Bull ordered him to do something, Toad jumped to obey. He wasn't very smart, but he was loyal to Bull. I believe the man could have asked anything of Toad, and he'd do his best to comply. Toad liked to talk though. He was full of stories. Most of them pretty gruesome."

"Tell me." Sam was far too eager for the kind of stories Toad provided, and Josh told her so.

She sniffed. "You can't blame me for wanting a bit of excitement."

He pushed her off balance so she tumbled in the snow. "That's the kind of excitement you need."

She righted herself and dusted the snow from her side. Then she turned and tackled him, sending him crashing into Katie. The three of them fell into a heap. Sam grabbed a handful of snow and scrubbed Josh's face with it.

"This enough excitement for you?" She giggled.

Katie extracted herself from the heap. "What has come over you two?"

Josh looked at Sam, raised his eyebrows, and tipped his head slightly toward Katie. Sam grinned, and the two of them rushed Katie. Josh caught her feet and prevented her from running away.

She squealed and tried to kick free, but Sam tossed snow at her and laughed.

Katie reached down and rubbed snow in Josh's face. He released her. She chased Sam until they both fell into the snow.

Josh got to his feet, jammed his fists on his hips, and pretended to glower at them. "Seems like cabin fever has followed you outside."

They lay side by side, laughing.

He jerked toward the downward trail and sniffed. "Do I smell smoke?" He sniffed again. "Come on. We need to see what it is."

The girls were instantly on their feet, grabbed their sacks, and the three of them trotted down the hill.

It wasn't long until they could see flames leaping from the roof of the cabin and licking down the sides.

"Nooo." Sam screamed and ran toward her home.

Josh caught her and stopped her. "You can't go inside. It's too late." She fought him a moment then collapsed into his arms, weeping quietly.

He caught Katie's hand, and the three of them clung together watching their home burn.

9

*K*atie wrapped her arms around Sam as she cried. Josh's arms circled them both. Katie leaned into his embrace as she watched the cabin become engulfed in flames. The heat forced them back as orange crawled down the walls. Flames wrapped around the window, and the glass fell to the ground and shattered. The door blackened as the heat seared it, and then it dissolved in flames.

Katie realized she was moaning and made herself stop.

They stood mesmerized as the cabin was reduced to charred logs and smoking ash. The stove stood like a wounded soldier in the midst of the devastation, a blackened log leaning on it.

Pulling Katie and Sam after him, Josh sank to the ground.

None of them spoke as they huddled together and stared at what was left of their home.

Josh let out a long breath. "There goes our shelter."

Katie didn't respond. What was there to say?

Sam clung to Josh's arm as it crossed over her stomach and simply stared. Her hat had fallen off, and Katie stroked her hair. "We're all safe. That's the most important thing." Although she believed it, she didn't sound totally convinced.

"And we have the woodshed, so we aren't completely without shelter," Josh added. "Once it cools off, we'll see if we can salvage the stove."

Katie tried for a laugh that sound suspiciously like a sob. "And we have supplies."

"That's right." Josh pushed them to their feet. "We have food in the shed, and because of Katie's idea of seeing what it was like to carry our sacks, we have some bedding."

"I have two books." Sam's voice rang with disgust. "What was I thinking?"

"At least you have something from your home." Josh pushed and pulled them toward the shed. "Come on. Let's get settled."

Inside the shed, they drew to a halt. "We have wood but no way of starting a fire." Josh shrugged. "I suppose we can light a fire from the hot embers of the cabin."

Katie studied the little enclosure. She hadn't realized how small it was. "Should we toss out some wood to make room for us?" Otherwise they would have to sleep standing up.

"Good idea. If we work together, it will be easy. Sam, you hand the logs to Katie. Katie, you stand here." Josh indicated the doorway. "And hand them to me. I'll stack them against the shed." He gazed at the smoldering cabin and shook his head. "We have to make the best of it."

It took them half an hour to make a spot barely big enough to accommodate them.

"Katie, you have a pot. We can heat water."

She bit her tongue to keep from saying she didn't want hot water. She wanted a warm house. "I have a frypan. I can heat up some of those rice and bean patties. We have fresh biscuits, thanks to you." Her voice grated, and she stopped before she could be reduced to tears.

"Sounds good. I'll start a fire." Josh went to the middle of the yard, well away from anything that might burn, and set out wood. He grabbed a shovel from the shed and fetched hot embers from the cabin. Soon a fire burned merrily.

Sam had not spoken a word for some time. Now she stood at the door of the shed, staring at the remains of her home.

Katie went to Josh where he watched the campfire and spoke softly. "She's awfully quiet."

"The child has lost everything apart from the few things we have with us. It's a shock."

"I'm worried about her."

Josh draped an arm about Katie's shoulders. She leaned into him. She could survive so long as he was there.

"I'm worried, too," he said. "Let's go talk to her."

"I don't know what to say."

"Anything at all, so long as she starts to listen and respond." He took Katie's hand and drew her toward Sam. "Sam, I'm sorry."

"Me, too." Katie tried to hug the girl, but she shrugged away. Katie bit back tears.

Josh leaned close to Sam. "I think I'm going to appreciate those rice and bean cakes you made. It's a good thing your pa taught you so many skills."

"I have no home. Nowhere to belong." Her voice shook with sorrow and perhaps a touch of bitterness.

Josh caught her chin and forced her to look at him. "Sam, you will have a home wherever I go. I promise you."

Hope flared in her eyes and then disappeared as quickly as if drowned by water thrown at her. "Until Bull finds you."

Katie gasped. The last thing they needed was to think of another disaster looming on their heels. "I pray he has given up. Taken us for dead."

Sam shrugged and went into the shed.

Katie closed her eyes and waited for calm to come from somewhere. Though she wondered if she would ever again feel safe.

Josh brushed his fingers along her cheeks. "I would say God directed you to think of taking things in our sacks today. He will continue to guide us."

She opened her eyes and looked into his, falling into the assurance he offered. "You aren't having any doubts?"

"God has kept me safe the past year in Bull's mine. He arranged for me to be there when you needed my help. He guided us here. Not only for our sake, but for Sam's. I'm not going to start doubting Him now."

His voice rang with conviction, and she nodded. "You might have to remind me again. And again."

His fingers rested on her face. "Gladly."

Sam came back out carrying patties. "Are we going to eat or not?"

"Yes." Katie broke away from Josh's touch and dug the frypan out of her sack.

Josh set two fresh pieces of wood over the fire that was now burned to hot coals.

Katie dropped the patties into the pan, and in a few minutes they were hot.

Josh lifted the pan to the side. "I'll pray while it cools enough to touch." He stood, his hat in his hand, and bowed his head.

Katie glanced at Sam before she bowed her own head.

Sam stared at the fire.

Katie wondered if she even heard Josh.

"Father God, thank You that we weren't in our beds when the cabin burned. Thank You we had supplies with us, and food stored in the shed. Thank You for food for supper and a shed to sleep in. Amen."

He glanced at Sam and then to Katie.

Katie shrugged.

Josh took out a patty and a biscuit and handed them to Sam. She shook herself and took them.

They ate in silence. Josh went to the pump and filled a canteen from the shed. Thankfully two had been stored there. He passed it around, and they all drank.

"Strange, isn't it?" Kate began, "How a fire can be so warm and inviting and yet do so much damage."

Sam shuddered. "Pa said a fire was our worst enemy. Now I understand what he meant."

Katie sat beside the girl. "Sam, if your pa was alive, what do you think he'd say right now?"

Sam snorted then burst into laughter. The laughter quickly gave way to sobs.

Katie wrapped her arms about the girl and held her.

Josh did the same on Sam's other side.

After a bit, Sam calmed.

"Pa would say some fool didn't check the stove before he left." She laughed again, a choked sound. "Pa would say a person pays for carelessness. Pa would say I got what I deserved."

"No. No." Josh was emphatic. "You don't have to be around this world long to realize that bad things happen to good people, and good things happen to those who don't deserve it."

Sam nodded. "I already seen that. It doesn't make sense."

"Neither does God's love, if you stop to think about it. We don't deserve it. Nor do we deserve the beauty of the mountains that we all enjoy. Yet it's there. We can ignore it. Keep our eyes on our feet. Or we can lift our heads and be touched by the beauty. Brings to mind a verse in the Psalms. 'I will both lay me down in peace, and sleep: for thou, Lord, only makest me dwell in safety.'"

"I guess it's true that God kept us from being burned to death in our sleep." Sam shuddered just as Katie did.

"Thank God for sparing any of us from being injured," Katie whispered.

Sam drew in a long breath. "I guess it could have been worse."

Josh chuckled. "That's a good way of looking at it. Why don't you ladies get out the quilts while I cover the fire? I wouldn't want it to get away on us. Here, take the fur." He took it off his shoulders and handed it to Katie.

She pressed it to her face as she and Sam went to the shed. It smelled of animal but also carried the memory of

Josh. The fur had kept her warm in the past. It would so in the future.

A future that appeared bleak at the moment.

She and Sam brushed aside the wood shavings until the dirt floor was clean. Sam fetched the quilts from the sacks. Katie stared at the tiny space. How were three of them to sleep there? They'd be crowded into one body. She closed her eyes, pushing away thoughts of what her parents would have said about her being in this situation with a man she wasn't married to.

She opened her eyes and kept them wide. She had no intention of freezing for the sake of propriety.

Josh ducked into the shed. The room was shrouded in darkness. "I don't suppose either of you thought to bring a candle."

Neither of them had.

"I'll leave the door open until we get a place ready. Where is the bedding?"

Katie handed him the fur and quilts. He spread a quilt on the ground. He put the second quilt against the wall to keep them from having their backs against the cold wood and held the fur open before him. "The only way all three of us will be covered is to crowd into it together. Ladies, settle in."

Katie made sure Sam was between her and Josh. She knew Josh got less of the covers than she did, but at the moment, all that mattered was keeping Sam warm and protected. "You'll be safer between us," she assured the girl.

Sam didn't argue.

Josh reached out and pulled the door closed, and darkness as thick as pudding surrounded them.

"My eyes quit working," Sam whispered.

"Look to your right." Josh's voice was so close Katie felt his breath in her hair. "See the moonlight peeking through that crack?"

Katie found the spot he meant. It was a tiny sliver of light, but it made her less afraid.

Sam must have found it too. "A finger of light." She seemed pleased.

"See, God hasn't forgotten us or abandoned us."

Sam sighed and relaxed. She must be pressed very tight to Josh's side, as Katie was sure she could feel his warmth reaching her. And his strength.

They were safe. Somehow, they would survive this.

JOSH KEPT the fur tightly around the girls even though it meant his back was exposed to the cold.

He had checked the stove before they left. He always did. But had he been careless? He reviewed every step. Told himself it wasn't his neglect that had caused the fire. Besides, what was done was done. Now they had to make the best of it.

His feet were cold. He shifted, trying to get them under the fur.

Sam mumbled something in her sleep.

Katie patted her and murmured, "You're safe."

Josh found Katie's hand in the dark and held it. She clung to him.

"Go to sleep," she murmured to him.

"I'm trying," he whispered. He would not admit aloud

that every time he closed his eyes flames danced in his vision.

He forced himself to lie motionless even though his body twitched to move. His mind raced at the reality of their loss.

He slipped from the little nest as soon as faint light crept through the cracks in the shed and hurried out to make a fire. The cabin still smoldered.

Katie emerged from the shed, Sam at her heels. They both paused to stare at the remains of their home then hurried to the fire and held out their hands.

"Did you sleep well?" he asked them. Both had cried out several times in their sleep.

"I kept dreaming I was trapped inside while it burned." Sam shuddered.

Katie hugged her. "I kept seeing the flames, and they were everywhere."

"We are all safe. That's the most important thing." Josh contemplated if he should make his announcement now or wait until after breakfast.

Katie brought out the last of the biscuits from yesterday and some dried meat.

Josh thanked God for food and safety, and they ate the food without any enthusiasm.

"We have to leave this place." He couldn't put off the matter. "We don't have enough food to last us long."

Katie stared at him. "It's winter."

"We are better prepared than when we left the mine." At least they had food enough for several days.

She nodded. The way she swallowed, Josh knew she understood the necessity. And the risks.

He turned to Sam, who stared at the remains of the cabin. "I know it's hard to think of leaving your home, but I don't see we have any choice."

Sam's shoulders rose and fell. She sniffled.

Josh went to her and gave her a sideways hug. "You can always come back for a visit at some point." Perhaps when she was older. And in better weather.

She swiped away the tears. Leaned her head to Josh's shoulder. "I'll say goodbye now." She left him and went to the smoldering ruins. She circled the cabin, pausing a time or two to kick at something on the ground. She stared at the twisted frames of the bed. Then, her jaw set in firm lines, she rejoined them. "Let's get out of here."

Josh had considered the need for a fire to keep them warm at night and the wild animals at bay, but he had no flint, no matches. "We'll have to survive without a fire."

"No fire?" Katie shivered.

"No matches. No flint."

Sam's eyes widened. "I just remembered something." She raced into the shed and emerged a moment later holding a flint. "Pa put one there."

"Your pa really believed in being prepared."

"Yup." She handed it to Josh.

That left the problem of wood. Could they find enough deadfall to see them through? He decided to take dry kindling in his sack. That would be the hardest thing to find. And the most necessary in getting a fire going.

They rolled up the quilts and put them in the girls' sacks again. He distributed the food among them. He filled the two canteens they had. They were ready. At the last minute, he decided to take the shovel. It might prove useful. He already had the axe hanging from his belt.

"Sam, which direction?" Though there was really only one way down the mountain. But he figured it would direct her thoughts away from her home if she had to be the guide.

They set out on the path he and Sam had created while trapping rabbits. They passed the trees and no longer had a trampled path to follow.

"I'll break trail," Josh said.

"Keep to the right." Sam pointed to a little draw that followed a hill.

He kept his steps short enough that both Sam and Katie could follow him in single file. It was hard work, but they had no choice but to press on. Sam had told him that with no snow, the trek might take three to four days. He figured fighting snow and whatever challenges they encountered would take five or more. They had enough food for five if they rationed it.

The sun was near its zenith when he saw a spot cleared by the wind on a nearby rise. "We'll stop there."

Katie and Sam let their sacks fall from their bodies and sank to the ground. Josh passed them a canteen.

Katie eyed it. "How long does this have to last?"

"We can melt snow over the fire when we stop for the night, so we'll be fine."

She nodded and drank then passed the canteen to Sam. Josh took a swig when she handed it to him then stopped the hole.

He got biscuits and rice and bean patties from his sack. "Ladies, may I interest you in our finest food?"

Katie's eyebrows rose, and Sam grunted, but they took the offered food and ate.

He wished he could let them rest longer, but the days were short. "We can rest when it gets dark." He got to his feet and held out his hands to help the pair up.

"At least the sun is shining," Katie murmured, looking around. "And the scenery is pretty."

"And we have a good guide." Josh grinned at Sam, who perked up. "Which way now?"

"We keep following this draw."

They went on for another hour. Conversation was reduced to a few words when needed. Otherwise, their energy and concentration were focused on hiking through the snow.

Soon the sun sank low. Trees cast long dark shadows across their way. It was time to find a place for the night. Josh stopped and glanced around.

"Something wrong?" Katie asked.

"We need a campsite."

Katie and Sam both straightened and scanned the area.

"What exactly are we looking for?" Katie asked.

"Ideally, there will be a little shack with a wood-burning stove inside, several soft beds, and a cook to serve us bacon and eggs."

That earned him scoffing laughter.

"But we'll settle for a flat place where we can build a fire. Trees nearby to stop the wind. Like that spot over there." He pointed, then led the way.

They helped him kick away the snow until the ground was relatively bare and scraped it cleaner still with the shovel. Even so, they would need protection from dampness, as the heat would cause the ground to get wet. They went to the trees to find deadwood for a fire. A few minutes later, they had a cheery blaze going.

"I'll be back in a minute or two." He meant to find pine boughs for bedding. He cut enough to make a comfortable bed. With so little bedding he only needed enough for one.

A set of tracks, barely visible in the snow, caught his attention. They belonged to a large animal. A mountain lion? He shuddered. But took comfort in the fact they were old tracks.

He returned to the campsite and got the bed organized while it was still light enough to see. They ate their sparse rations. Neither of the others seemed inclined to conversation. Likely as tired as he was.

Yet he felt he needed to offer some words of encouragement. "My pa, the preacher, always used every occasion as a reminder of what God was doing."

Two pairs of eyes came to his, waiting for him to continue. He smiled to know he'd caught their interest.

"I was thinking what he might say about this and remembered a story he liked to tell. I will tell it to you as I remember it." He cleared his throat dramatically, and Sam giggled. "Once upon a time there was a farmer with one son. He adored this son and planned his entire life around him. They had a mare that they used to get back and forth to town. One day, the mare was stolen. 'That's bad,' the father said. Now they had no way of getting to town. But a neighbor learned of their plight and offered to sell them a young mare who was in foal. The father looked at the mare. She had fine form, and he spent his last penny to get the horse. The foal was healthy and strong. 'Our bad has brought good,' the father said to the son. 'We have a better horse than we had before.' As the foal matured, the son began to work with it. One day, he decided it was time to break the young horse for riding."

Josh paused.

Sam leaned forward. "What you're saying is the bad turned out to be good."

"Seems that way, doesn't it. But there's more."

Katie nudged him. "Then let's hear it."

He chuckled. "The young horse did not want to be ridden and tossed the son to the ground. His leg was badly broken, so he could never walk properly again." He didn't realize he rubbed his leg that had been shot until Katie spoke.

"Does your leg still hurt?"

"Only occasionally." When he overused it.

She edged closer so she could squeeze his arm. "I think hiking through the snow bothers it."

Sam sat close on the other side, as if the two of them needed to be near him. "So, the good turned into bad?" she asked.

Josh continued. "That's what the son said. But a few months later, soldiers came for young men to draft into the army. The son with his weak leg was of no interest to them. The father had learned his lesson. He said, 'What I thought was bad was really for our good. I should have never doubted God's love and care.' The end."

Sam sighed. "It's hard to see the good when you're in the bad."

"That's true. But God sees the end. We trust Him."

"I wish it *was* the end." Sam said.

Josh wished they were safely in the town of Glory.

"Let's get some sleep. Sam, you go in the middle again. Katie and I will be on either side of you." They got as comfortable as they could. He made sure the fur covered them. But he planned to keep the fire going. Any wild animals would shy away from the flames, and they would be safe.

His nerves prickled with the sensation that dozens of slanted green eyes peered from the trees. Next time, he'd camp far from trees even if it meant he had to fetch wood from a mile away.

10

_K_atie woke up in an instant. Her neck hurt. Sam crowded close. The fur enclosed them both. Where was Josh? Fear jolted through her. Were they alone in the snow-encased vastness?

She lifted her head. Josh squatted by the fire.

She let her breath out slowly. Of course, he wouldn't leave her…them. She knew that as surely as she knew her name. Easing out of the warm cocoon, leaving Sam covered, she hurried to join Josh at the fire.

"Morning," he said.

"I see we survived the night."

He chuckled softly. "Did you have doubts about it?"

She grinned. "None at all. We will make it out." She studied him. Lines that weren't normally there fanned out from his eyes. "Didn't you sleep?"

"A little." Seeing her concern, he added, "I'm fine."

"What kept you from sleeping?"

His laugh rang with mocking. "Nothing really. The

cold, worry, concern about getting us all to safety. Like I said. Nothing really."

Did he realize his gaze had darted to the stand of trees and lingered there? And his worry lines had deepened?

"What did you see in the trees?"

He jerked his attention to the fire and didn't meet her gaze. "Nothing out of the ordinary."

An answer she did not find comforting. Mountain lions could be expected in this area. Recalling the growl of the one who had been so close when they escaped Bull, she shivered.

Josh might think he was protecting her and Sam by not telling them if he saw anything of concern. That was all well and good. Very noble on his part. But she'd sooner be informed and ready.

"I need to make a trip into the trees. For privacy." She followed the path he had made, carefully studying the ground. There were some deep prints that must have belonged to an animal. From the space between them, she knew it had to be a larger animal. She could tell the prints were old, so she wasn't concerned. But she would be careful to watch for any other signs

She heard Sam talking to Josh and returned to the campsite.

They were all anxious to be on their way and ate a quick breakfast, filled the canteens with the melted snow, repacked everything, and were on their way.

In a couple of hours, Josh stopped. Katie and Sam joined him to see why. Before them the trees closed in. It would be difficult to go that direction. A rugged hill rose to the other side.

"Which way?" Josh asked Sam.

Sam's brow wrinkled in concentration. And worry. "It looks different with all the snow." She turned full circle. "I don't remember."

Katie stilled the alarm choking her. If they were lost, how long would they wander aimlessly?

"We'll figure it out." Josh sounded calm. But then, it seemed nothing upset him. "See that rock outcropping?" He directed Sam's gaze that direction. "Does it seem familiar?"

"Maybe. Maybe we climbed the hill there and went around the trees."

Katie wished for something a little more reassuring. Josh must have sensed her worry, for he squeezed her shoulder. "From what Sam has said, we know we have to go down the mountain and to the south."

She nodded, pushing aside the protest that there was a lot of land to the south of where they stood.

"Let's go back and climb that hill."

"I'm sorry." Sam's words had a liquid sound to them as if tears built behind them.

"We're doing all right," Josh said, smiling at the girl. "Let's not forget that we are not alone."

Katie jerked her head up and scanned the surrounding area. "I don't see anyone. Nor do I want to."

Josh pointed upward. "We are not alone."

His reminder and his confidence calmed her. "Let's find the way."

His grin of approval filled her heart. They retraced their steps to where Josh decided they would start climbing. The slope wasn't steep, but she soon discovered it was difficult to tell what was under her feet. They passed a rocky outcrop, climbed a little more, and reached the crest of the hill. They stopped to catch their breath.

Josh studied the land before them. "Let's head for that draw. We'll stay on the hill, so we aren't in deep snow."

Onward they marched. Katie could understand why Sam didn't recognize any landmarks. Everything looked the same under the mantle of snow.

Josh again stopped. "Let's have something to eat." He indicated the nearby rocks and they sat on them to rest though the cold soon penetrated their clothes. They settled for leaning against the rocks as they ate dried meat and biscuits.

Katie would have liked to have eaten more but understood the need to ration their food.

They moved on. The ground before them grew less rocky, and they could see for miles down the slope. But she recognized it was too steep for them to navigate. They would have to stay on the rocky mountainside.

Sam gasped. "I know where we are. We shouldn't be here. Pa warned me this was dangerous." Her words came out in bullet-like blasts. She pointed to the left. "That's where Bull has his mine."

Katie's throat closed off. Bull? How close were they? The skin on her face tightened. The landscape shivered. She realized she had grown dizzy and forced herself to take a breath.

"Then we'll go the opposite direction." Josh's voice crackled. He looked to Katie. Must have seen her fright. "Are you all right?"

"I will be when we get away from here." Her teeth chattered.

He pulled her closer. Planted his hands on her shoulders and tipped his forehead to hers. "Lord, God, guide us. Protect us."

She reached for his hands and held tightly to them. His touch almost caused her to believe she was safe. But if Bull…

She straightened. "Let's get away from here."

"I'm sorry." Sam choked out the words. "It's my fault."

Josh pulled her close, into a three-cornered hug. "It's not your fault. We are not alone in this. Remember what God says: 'When thou passest through the waters, I will be with thee; and through the rivers, they shall not overflow thee: when thou walkest through the fire, thou shalt not be burned; neither shall the flame kindle upon thee.' He is with us. Now let's get out of here."

He led the way down the hill and toward the right. But 'getting out of here' seemed to take a long time. Katie glanced back over her shoulder. Anyone standing on the hill opposite would easily see them.

Something in the distance moved. She squinted to make it out.

"Josh." She couldn't explain why she kept her voice low. They were too far away to be overheard. "Josh." Her voice rose.

He came to her side. "What?"

She pointed. "Do you see it?"

He stared. "It's a man on horseback. Coming this way."

He didn't need to say anything more. If it wasn't Bull, it was almost certainly someone following his orders.

Katie turned and ran, resenting the snow that slowed her. Sam ran too, a moan escaping her lips.

JOSH HURRIED AFTER THE PAIR, caught them, and forced them to stop. "You're wasting your time and energy. I'll lead the way." A mountainous slope rose to the right. So, he went to the left and made his way downward, seeking a place where the snow wasn't so deep. He found what might have been a trail of sorts. The footing was better. In places, the snow had blown away, and they were able to go faster.

"He's gaining on us." Katie's voice was shrill.

"We might find a place to hide." He didn't really think so but had to offer some hope.

The trail descended. He decided it was faster if they followed it. His foot slipped, and he gasped at how close he'd come to falling down the slope. He must be careful. One misstep could end in disaster. "Mind your footing," he called over his shoulder. The glance allowed him to see that the rider was closing the distance between them. He couldn't make out the man's features, but from his bulky size, he guessed it to be Bull.

Sam and Katie had both paused to glance back.

Sam whimpered. "He's going to catch us."

"Not if I can help it. Let's keep going." They struggled onward. Their breathing grew labored.

"Josh," Katie called. The fear in her voice stopped him cold, and he slowly turned.

Bull had reached the bottom of his side and now only had to cross the narrow draw and follow their wide trail.

"You can't get away," he bellowed over the distance. "I'll be taking all of you back." He chortled. A nasty, frightening sound.

Sam grabbed Josh's arm. "He'll find out I'm a girl. I'm afraid."

Josh had always wondered if Daniel had been afraid in the lion's den. At that moment, he was convinced the man had been. He had determined to obey God even if it cost him his life. God had rescued him. But others had trusted God in death. Josh vowed he would too.

"I will not let him take us." If only the rifle hadn't been destroyed in the fire.

"How will you stop him?" Kate's voice shook so hard he could barely make out her words.

"I'm trusting God to provide a way."

Bull's horse struggled in the deep snow. "I'm coming. Can't wait to have my fun." He roared with laughter.

A roar of rolling thunder followed his mocking laughter. They glanced at the sky. It was clear blue. Besides, there weren't thunderstorms in the winter. The ground shook.

Katie and Sam grabbed his arms.

"What is it?" Kate cried.

"I don't know." A huge cloud of snow billowed off the side of the mountain. "It's an avalanche! Run!" They turned, and he ran, praying his feet would find solid footing and that the girls could keep up. Snow sprinkled over them. And then all was quiet.

Afraid of what he would discover, he turned. Sam stared at him with eyes so wide he wondered if she would be able to close them again.

Katie met his gaze, fear blazing from her eyes. Slowly, she turned.

Before them, where there had once been a valley,

there was now a swath of white with puffy snow clouds hovering over it.

He and Sam went to Katie's side and stared.

Sam asked the question that was surely uppermost in all their minds. "Where's Bull?"

"I don't know." They watched for several minutes, as if expecting horse and rider to emerge from the snow.

They didn't.

"Bull might have escaped. He might be safe on the other side. But I don't think he'll be following us any time soon."

He held Katie and Sam tight to his side as he offered a prayer of gratitude.

It seemed none of them could dredge up the energy to move on. "We can't stay here," he said after a bit. "There's no place to camp."

They turned and trudged onward. Just when it seemed they would cling forever to the side of the mountain, the trail ended. Before them lay a flat area, bordered by trees. "We'll stop there."

Remembering his vow to avoid being too close to trees, he chose a spot by some boulders that would break the wind. They again swept the snow off the ground. He left them to finish the task while he went to find wood. There was plenty of deadfall, and he returned with a full armload and went back several times to ensure they had a supply to last the night.

Then he went to find boughs to sleep on. His leg ached, and he rubbed it. He couldn't wait to return to Verdun and get some of his ma's liniment.

"Josh?" Katie's voice felt close.

He turned. She was only a few steps away.

"I've come to help." She crossed to him, wrapped her arms around him, and held him tight. "I have never been so scared in my life. I thought we were all going to die."

He held her, leaned his face against her head, and breathed in the scent of her.

"You know what it reminded me of?" Her voice was muffled against him.

"What?"

"The Egyptians following the Israelites through the Red Sea and how the water closed in over them. God truly save us."

They held each other. He guessed the whole incident had left her as shaken as it had him. It was gruesome to think of Bull and his horse being buried under tons of snow. But perhaps he had escaped. That idea wasn't any more comforting than the previous one.

"Where are you guys?" Sam's voice made Josh release Katie, although reluctantly. He found it comforting to hold her.

"Hello? Have you forgotten me? I'm here all alone."

"We're coming," he called. He gathered up the boughs he'd cut, and Katie accompanied him back to the camp.

"I was getting scared." Sam's voice wobbled.

He dropped the boughs where they would sleep and pulled Sam to his side, pressing her head to the hollow of his shoulder. "We didn't mean to frighten you."

Her voice was muffled. "I know."

Katie joined Josh in hugging the girl.

It might not be acceptable by people living safe and warm in their houses for him to be holding these two, but things were different here. It was the three of them against a vast white wilderness. They had to encourage each other.

They broke apart and ate the sparse food. He chewed the meat slowly. Needed a swallow of water to get it down. "I thought dried meat was a good idea."

"It's keeping us alive." Katie almost choked on her mouthful. "The patties are a better idea, but they tend to fall apart."

"Too bad Pa isn't here. He'd find us some fresh game and roast it over the fire."

"Stop." Katie held up her hand. "You're making my mouth water."

"All the better for getting this food down." Sam's voice was so droll that Josh laughed. Katie chuckled too. His gaze met hers and lingered there.

When she smiled, soft and slow, something warm brushed his soul. He couldn't think of anyone he'd sooner be with in such a time.

The smoke drove him from his side of the fire. The three of them sat together on the cushiony bed though none of them made any move toward actually going to bed.

"Tell us more stories." Sam leaned against his arm.

He shifted so he could put his arm around her. It felt perfectly normal to put his other arm around Katie. "What sort of stories?"

"About your family." Sam's voice was achingly wistful, as if she wanted to enjoy the sort of life she'd never had.

"You've heard about all my sisters." He told them how each had come to the family. "Flora was such a wild thing. Eve just the opposite. Always trying to keep everyone safe. I remember once….." He proceeded with a tale.

A little later, he grew silent. "Aren't you ladies sleepy?"

"Not me." Sam pulled a quilt across her legs. "It's nice here."

"Katie? Are you ready to go to bed?"

"I agree with Sam. It's nice right here." She chuckled; a low, pleasant sound that made Josh agree that it was nice sitting here.

"Besides," Katie continued. "Technically, we are on the bed."

"True." They sank into quiet contemplation of the flames.

Sam shivered.

"Are you cold?"

"No. Just thinking." She turned so she could see Josh and Katie. "We were almost buried in that avalanche."

"I remember another story. It's about a man who lost almost everything. His little son died. He lost his business. He sent his wife and four daughters to Europe, planning to follow later. There as an accident at sea and the four girls perished. Only his wife survived. Later, he crossed the ocean to join her. When they passed the spot where the girls had died, he wrote a beautiful hymn. My pa learned it." He cleared his throat and began to sing "It is Well With My Soul."

He finished. Both the girls relaxed against him.

"That was nice." Katie sounded half asleep. "Sing some more."

"You sure you don't mind listening to me?" His modesty was only for show. He knew he had a good singing voice. His parents had often had him sing in church, many times with one or more of his sisters.

Katie jabbed her elbow into his ribs. "You have a nice voice, which I'm sure you know."

He chuckled. "I do know a few hymns, what with me being the preacher's son and all."

"Stop talking and sing," Sam said with a touch of impatience.

Smiling, he did exactly that. He sang until the fire had died down to glowing embers then eased the drowsy pair to lie down on the bed. "I need to put on more wood."

A few minutes later, he lay down beside Sam, tucked the fur more tightly across Katie.

She caught his hand and held it.

They were safe. Sheltered by God's love and care. Tomorrow would take them that much closer to a town.

Things would be different when they reached safety.

He would be glad of that, but there might be changes he would regret.

⸺⸺⸺⸺

$\mathcal{T}$he next day Katie rose, ready to face whatever challenges they encountered.

"Sing that song again," she said to Josh as they ate breakfast.

"'It is Well With My Soul'?"

"Yes. It makes me believe I am safe."

He sang, his gaze holding hers as he did. She didn't even try to look away. A glow of sunshine rose in the eastern sky and bathed him in brightness. Assurance filled her, fueled by the words of the song and the comfort of Josh's voice.

Sam began to pack her sack.

Katie realized the song had ended. It was time to be on their way.

They left the campsite and headed down the slope. For a time, the way was relatively easy despite the snow that crunched under their feet. Then they had to make their way through some trees. They were on the other side of them in time for the noon break. Before them lay a rocky incline.

Sam waved her hands. "I remember this. We climb it, and in a short time we'll come to a little lake. It was real nice in the summertime."

They ate their rations and rested for a few minutes then were climbing the rugged surface. It was a good thing Sam had assured them it wasn't a long trek, because the footing was treacherous. Unable to see what lay beneath the snow, Josh tested every step. Even so, Katie's foot often slipped off a rock.

Josh stopped and glanced back to make sure Katie and Sam were all right. "We've almost reached the top."

But once they did so, Katie realized the descent was every bit as treacherous. They made their way between boulders and along narrow passages. If any of them stumbled, they would have a nasty fall.

Please keep us safe. Protect us. Guide our feet. Katie repeated the words over and over in her head.

Sam's scream drew Katie's attention from watching where she put her foot.

She stared as Josh went down, falling against a rock as he landed. Thankfully he was away from steepest part of the ledge.

He lay there. Sam was at his side in an instant, and Katie followed.

Josh sat up. Although he tried to hide it, she saw pain in his eyes. She knelt at his side. "Are you injured?"

The way he sucked in air told her that the pain went deep. "I don't think so."

She helped him up.

He straightened slowly, grimacing, and leaned over to

rub his leg. "Nothing broken. I'm all right." But the smile he gave to reassure them twisted to one side.

Sam's face crumpled. "You could have gone over the edge. Maybe died." Her voice grew high and thin.

Josh drew her to his side. "I didn't, and I'm all right. We're all right. Let's get off this hill."

"I'll break trail," Katie said.

Josh paled. "No. I know what I'm doing. Besides, look at your footwear."

She didn't need to. Her boots were too thin by far and barely kept her feet dry, let alone warm. But she would not mention it. There was nothing any of them could do but keep going. She stepped aside and let him lead the way.

Because his back was to them, she couldn't see his face but guessed he grimaced with every step. He might have tried to hide it, but he limped.

How badly had he hurt his leg?

They reached a flat area, passed through a narrow band of trees, and came to the lake Sam had mentioned and which they'd had glimpses of from the hill they'd crossed.

"It's a perfect place to camp for the night," Katie called.

Josh led them to a spot just past the trees and dropped his sack.

She could see his face for the first time since he'd fallen. Beneath the ruddy color from the cold, there was an unmistakable grayish hue. She bit her lip to keep from mentioning it.

She and Sam cleaned the snow of the chosen spot while Josh went to get wood.

Sam waited until he was out of sight. "He hurt himself, didn't he?"

"I'm afraid so."

"How bad is it?"

She wished she could assure the girl that it was nothing to be concerned about, but Sam was far too smart for that. "I don't know, and he won't likely say. But we can pray he's able to go on."

Sam drew her lips in. Tears flooded her eyes. "What happens if he can't?"

"Do you think we can carry him out?" Katie tried to sound teasing, but knew she'd failed.

"At least we are over the roughest part of the trail."

Josh returned with a load of wood, and they lit the fire. When he headed back to the trees, both Katie and Sam followed.

"We'll help," Katie said.

The fact that he didn't protest proved to Katie how much pain he endured.

He chopped pine boughs while Katie and Sam gathered deadwood. Their arms full, they returned to the fire. Josh sank to the boughs as soon as they were in place.

Katie knelt in front of him. "Josh, how bad is it? Be honest with me."

"It hurts, but nothing's broken. It will be fine after a night's rest."

"Then you are going to rest. Sam and I will take care of everything." Not that there was a lot to do. Throw wood on the fire as needed. Fill the pot with snow to get water. Eat their rations. "It's a nice spot." She took in the sight. The lake was flat. In spots the ice was blown clear, and the setting sun lit it gold and red. After seeing rocks and ridges, the levelness was a pleasure to behold.

The food was stowed away, and then by silent mutual consent she and Sam sat on either side of Josh, holding his hands and sharing their body heat. Knowing he was in no mood to talk or sing, Katie said, "I remember when my father was alive and the outings he took me on." She remembered things she had almost forgotten. Special times. Happy times. And she relayed them.

"It sounds nice," Sam said when Katie grew silent.

"I think it's time to go to bed." She arranged the bedding. Sam lay down first with Katie on one side of her and Josh on the other. "I'll tend the fire." Katie's words were firm.

"I can do it." Josh sounded weary.

"What you can do is rest that leg. I'll do it."

"Very well. I don't have the energy to argue."

"Good. Because I do."

His snort was half laugh. "Good night, Katie. Good night, Sam."

Katie waited until his breathing deepened to slide the fur over and cover him completely. Immediately she realized how cold it was and pressed closer to Sam.

After a few minutes she slipped from the bed and went to the fire where it was warmer. She hunkered down on one of the sacks, adding more wood as needed.

One side of her was hot. The other cold and she turned about. At what she saw she almost stepped back into the fire.

A pair of slanted yellow eyes peered at her from outside the circle of light.

Her heart slammed into her ribs. A mountain lion. So close.

Anger, sudden and raw, like a raging fire, raced through her veins.

No mountain lion was going to harm her sleeping family.

She grabbed a burning branch and ran toward the animal, jabbing the fire toward the eyes. They disappeared.

With the burning torch held high, she took a good look around and circled the fire to make sure the intruder wasn't coming at them from a different direction. Satisfied it had fled, she tossed the branch back on the fire and moved the sack to the end of the bed of boughs and sat there. Every few minutes she rose and studied the area to make sure the animal hadn't returned.

The night deepened. The ice on the lake creaked and cracked. Nearby, an owl hooted. Katie's head drooped over her chest.

A noise jerked her awake and set her heart into a frantic race.

She grabbed a torch and circled the perimeter of the fire. The noise came again. She lowered the torch. Josh groaned in his sleep.

She held the firebrand to one side and leaned over him.

His eyes opened, dull with pain.

"Josh. What can I do to help?"

"Nothing. It's just a bruise."

"It's on the leg where you were shot, isn't it?" She was guessing, but figured she was right.

"Yeah." His voice rasped.

She jabbed the torch into the snow, far enough away to pose no threat yet close enough to provide some illumination, and sat beside Josh. "Would it help to put ice on it?"

"I'm already cold."

Sam stirred and snuggled closer to him.

Katie was half tempted to curl up on the other side of him. Protect him. Keep him warm. But thoughts of a big cat out there convinced her otherwise. She pulled the fur around him and tucked it in place.

"You'll be cold," he protested.

"I'll stay close to the fire." She had another look around then took the torch back to the fire. For some time, she stood there, turning one way and then the other to keep warm. She listened for Josh. He moaned and shifted on the boughs.

She felt so helpless. What could she do except pray for him?

God, this is a bad thing that happened to Josh. I don't know what good can come of it. All I ask is for him to be all right and for us to get to safety soon.

The words of the song Josh had sung several times calmed her. *It is well with my soul.* God was with them through good and bad.

Weary from the exertions of the day, she sat with her back to the bed, facing the fire. Although she tried to stay awake, she couldn't.

The cold wakened her. It was still dark out. The fire had burned to embers.

Fear further iced her veins, and she jumped up to check for a mountain lion. Seeing none, she tossed wood on the fire. As soon as the flames leaped up, she went to Josh. He still moaned and tossed and turned. How bad was his leg? Would he be able to keep walking?

MORNING FINALLY CAME and with it, renewed fears as Josh almost collapsed when he tried to stand.

She rushed to his side, but he waved her away.

"I'm fine." He limped into the trees.

"He's not fine." Sam stared after him. "He thrashed about all night."

"I know." Katie made up her mind. "Sam, we're going to stay here for the day and let him rest."

"But—"

"He won't make it if we go on now. And I won't leave him."

Sam stared at her; eyes wide with shock. "I wouldn't either."

"I know." She looked around. "This is a good place to stay." Apart from the predatory cat, but she wouldn't mention that to anyone. As soon as Josh returned, she told him of their decision.

"We have to keep moving," he protested.

"You said yourself that your leg just needed rest. That's what it will get today. Besides, we've been pushing hard, and could all use a break before we move on."

Sam brightened. "I can fish. Pa taught me how."

Glad that the girl was enthused about something, Katie admitted she would love some fresh fish.

Josh sat on the quilts, his hands hanging between his knees. "I don't like being the cause of delay."

She chuckled. "I wondered what good could come of

this, but if it means we will enjoy something different to eat, I'm going to believe that's it."

Sam set to work as soon as she'd eaten her rations. She took the ax and went to the edge of the lake to cut willow saplings. Needing to warm them up, she came back to the fire and began making something that looked like a basket.

Katie said she would see if she could find anything useful. She went the direction she had seen the cat eyes glaring at her. The tracks were there, so she hadn't imagined it. She could see where it had crouched to watch her. More tracks revealed it had run toward the lake. After following the tracks for a distance, she was convinced it had fled the area.

She picked up an armload of deadwood on her way back in case Josh questioned why she had gone so far.

But he lay curled on his side on the boughs, wrapped in the fur.

Sam had gone to the lake and was chopping a hole in the ice.

Katie put her load of wood on the ground and went to Josh's side so she could see his face. He tried to smile, but it was more of a grimace.

She sat beside him, careful not to bump his leg. "It's not getting any better, is it?"

"No. But it's not getting any worse. We'll be leaving tomorrow morning. You can count on it."

She rubbed his arm, wishing she could hold him and somehow help bear his pain.

"Don't you worry about me. I just happened to bang it at the same place Bull shot me."

Anger flared through her. She regretted sparing a sad

thought for the idea of Bull buried in the avalanche. She hoped he was.

"I had to continue working while it healed. Guess it never got really strong again."

She continued to rub his arm until he caught her hand and held it next to his heart. "You're going to regret having me along."

She turned to her knees and faced him. "Josh, I can't think of anyone I'd sooner be here with. You rescued me from Bull. You kept me warm and safe as we fled into the woods. You sang and told stories that have kept our spirits up."

He cupped his hand to the back of her head and drew her closer. "Katie, I want you to know something—" His gaze searched her face as if memorizing every line. She did the same with him.

"Look what I got." Sam's yell jerked Katie away from whatever Josh had been about to say. Sam held aloft three fish, and although Katie's mouth watered at the promise of fresh food, she wished Sam had waited two more minutes. Long enough for Josh to finish and maybe...even maybe... kiss her.

At the audacity of her thoughts, her cheeks burned, and she hurried over to join Sam.

JOSH COULD HAVE KICKED HIMSELF, except it hurt too much to move. It had to be his pain that had prompted him to draw Katie close. He'd been about to tell her how much he cared for her. Had even considered kissing her. Thankfully, Sam had intruded before he could embarrass

Katie any more than he had. Her bright red cheeks had told on her.

The pain in his leg was familiar. The same as when he'd been shot and then been forced to work as it healed. Only it had never healed properly. Bull saw to that.

The fall on the rock had broken the skin. Blood soaked his long johns but didn't darken his trousers. He was grateful for that. At least Katie wouldn't have to know. A rest for the day might help. Or it might not. Either way they had to push on tomorrow. Even with fish added to their diet, their food wouldn't last much longer.

The smell of frying fish brought him from a nap, and he sat up, swallowing back a groan as his leg reminded him of his recent accident.

They had no eating utensils and only one pan, but Katie and Sam had found sticks and sharpened them. He sat on the edge of the bed and joined them in spearing bites of fish.

"Not bad," he said.

Katie gave him a wide-eyed, surprised look. "I'd say it's excellent."

"Isn't that what I said? Doesn't not bad mean good?" He did his best to appear confused, but at the way Katie and Sam shook their heads as if saddened by his behavior, he knew he had not fooled them.

Katie studied him hard. "Nice to see you're well enough to tease. Is your leg any better?"

"It's improving." But as soon as the fish was gone, he needed to make a trip to the woods. Was it possible to wait until the girls were diverted so they wouldn't watch him? "Sure is a nice view," he said, pointing to the lake. But they only gave it a glance.

He grew suspicious. Were they purposely hanging about to see how well he could walk? Very well, if that's how it was. "I need to go." He pointed to the trees, gathered up every bit of resolve he could muster and made his way that direction congratulating himself that he barely limped.

As soon as he was out of sight, he grabbed the nearest tree and clung to it, sweat beading his forehead. He was half tempted to stay hidden in the trees where he could moan and groan as much as he wanted. But Katie would search for him if he was too long, so he finished his business and went back to the campsite, managing to control his pain when he came into view.

It encouraged him to know he could do so. He'd rest today then resume the journey tomorrow. No matter what.

Sam spent the afternoon fishing. They fried up half a dozen fish at suppertime, setting aside three for breakfast. He was a little concerned that the aroma might attract animals but reasoned that if they kept the fire burning brightly, the predators would stay away.

Katie must have thought the same thing because she brought in load after load of deadwood.

She refused to lie down at bedtime, saying she would watch the fire.

He wanted to argue. Say he would get up and tend it. But the look of warning in her eyes silenced him.

Sam wanted to know why he chuckled as they wrapped themselves in the fur.

"Because Katie is so cute when she's bossy."

Sam laughed. "Better not let her hear you say that."

"I won't. You can count on it."

HE ROUSED THE NEXT MORNING, aware he had slept much better than the night before. His leg still hurt, but it was bearable. He slipped from the bed. Sam still slept. Katie had curled up on two sacks. The fire had burned down. He added wood and stirred it to life then trekked into the woods.

Today they would move on. His leg was strong enough.

After eating the fish and a biscuit each, they packed up.

"Which way, Sam?" he asked.

"Around the lake to the left. Seems to me we will be getting close to where people live."

They set out. For a bit, they walked the trail Katie had made gathering wood and then fresh, untouched snow lay before them.

"We'll take turns breaking trail." Katie pushed past him. "My turn first."

"And then mine," Sam said.

"You're ganging up on me. That's not fair."

"It's because we don't fancy having to carry you out." Sam grinned at him then followed Katie, leaving him to bring up the rear.

"Well, if that's how you feel about it." He tried to sound hurt, but in truth, it pleased him to think they cared that much. Besides, being in the rear, he could rub his leg and limp as much as he wanted…needed.

An hour later, he was grateful to be following a

broken trail. His leg felt like someone had jabbed a spear into it and then twisted it out of sheer meanness. Something Bull would delight in doing. How many times had he walked past Josh and slammed his fist into the wound? Sometimes using a shovel or something sharp. To remind Josh what happened to men who tried to escape. He couldn't wait to make it back to Verdun and get some of Ma's healing compounds on that wound.

They stopped for a break and to eat. He sank to the ground, not even caring that he sat in snow. He turned his injured leg into the cold, hoping it would numb the pain.

Katie hovered beside him as they ate their meager rations. "We can rest here." The worry in her voice caused Josh to suck back the pain and push to his feet.

"The days are short, and we've already wasted one because of your worry." His words were unnecessarily sharp. He might have pulled them back at the wounded look in Katie's face, but wasn't sure he could make his voice gentle. "It's my turn to lead." Gritting his teeth, he set out. The lake was still to their right. Trees crowded in on the left. How far before they reached the open plains and easier travel?

His jaw muscles protested at how tight he clenched his teeth. Ahead, the trees spread apart, providing him a glimpse of rolling hills. No more mountains to scale or narrow paths to follow along rocky precipices. He couldn't take his eyes off the promising view.

He knew better. The path before him required his attention.

But the warning came too late. His feet went out from under him on a patch of ice he would have seen if he hadn't been distracted. He waved his arms madly, trying to regain control.

"Josh!" Katie's alarm rang through the air. Sam added her voice.

He couldn't get his feet back under him and crashed to the ground. The snow had been blown into sharp protrusions. A searing pain ripped through his leg.

12

*K*atie rushed to Josh's side. "Your leg!" He'd been limping since they'd left their noon break. This fall would surely make it worse.

"I'm fine." He pressed his mittened hand to his leg and closed his eyes.

She knew he sucked back pain. "Let me see it." Though with his trousers on, there was little to see. Nevertheless, she lifted his hand and gasped at the dark spot growing on his leg. "Josh, you're bleeding. Oh, Josh."

Sam knelt on Josh's other side. "Is it broken?"

Josh tried to sit up. Katie helped him though everything in her protested that he needed to rest. "It's not as bad as it looks. The gunshot wound never fully healed, and my fall broke it open again."

Katie sat with her shoulder to Josh's, holding him upright. "Wasn't that months ago? Why hasn't it healed?"

A furrow appeared across Josh's forehead, and his lips drew back. "Bull knew I couldn't try and get away if my leg was hurt."

Katie gasped when she realized what Josh meant. "What did he do? No. Don't tell me. I don't want to have such pictures in my mind."

An explosive noise came from Sam, and she bolted to her feet and walked away.

Katie and Josh watched her.

"Help me to my feet," Josh whispered.

"Your leg."

"We can't stay here."

Seeing he meant to get up one way or another, she helped him.

The dark area on his trousers widened.

"Ignore it. We have to move on."

He was right on one score. They couldn't stay here with no shelter and almost no food. And wild animals roaming in the area.

But he almost collapsed again when he put weight on his injured leg.

"Wait. I'll get you a cane to lean on." She held her hand out for the ax then went into the trees. The branch would have to be sturdy and straight. It took her a few minutes to find something that she deemed appropriate and a few more to chop it down, then she took it to him.

"Thanks." His voice was thin, indicating his pain.

Sam went first, breaking trail. Katie followed Josh, prepared to spring to his aid.

Their progress was slow as Josh struggled with each step.

"We're almost past the lake." Katie hoped it would provide encouragement for Josh. "We'll take a break as soon as we are."

Josh's only reply was a grunt.

Katie estimated it took them an hour to reach the end of the lake. They drew to a stop and gazed at the hills before them promising easier travels.

Josh sank to the ground. His face was wet with sweat, and he shivered though he tried to hide it. The dark spot on his trousers that started at his thigh had gone almost to the top of his boots.

Katie sat beside him while Sam hovered nearby shifting from one foot to the other.

"We need help." Her voice was shrill.

Katie couldn't agree more, but no one knew where they were. She gave a short, mirthless laugh. *They* didn't even know where they were.

"My help comes from the Lord." Josh spoke softly, certainly. His words soothed Katie. But were they supposed to sit there and wait for God to send rescue? That hardly made sense. But neither was it possible for Josh to continue. He had barely been able to make the last ten steps.

"Pray."

She jerked around to stare at Josh. His eyes were dark, pain-filled, but even deeper was his calm assurance.

"Pray," he said again.

She nodded.

"Out loud." His words were firm, demanding...inviting.

"Me?" It wasn't something she was comfortable with.

"I need you to." His voice grew thin, as if it cost him the last of his energy to speak them.

She could hardly refuse his request. "Very well." She bowed her head and collected her thoughts. Josh had been their strong support, reminding them of God's care and protection. She'd leaned on his strength. Now it was time to offer hers. And she would. "God in heaven, You see us. You know where we are. You know, too, that Josh can't go on. So, we sit here trusting You to guide us. Whatever happens, our lives are in Your care. Amen."

Josh reached for her hand and reached for Sam's on his other side. The three of them sat pressed together, looking down the valley. Whatever happened, they were together.

The scattered clouds that had filled the sky blew away, leaving white horsetails brushing the blue ceiling. Did the others feel as peaceful as she? They had done all they could.

She studied the land before them. So calm and peaceful, disturbed by nothing man-made, though at the moment she would love to see a factory spewing out smoke or a wagon trundling along a road. Even smoke rising from a chimney.

She blinked. Her imagination was getting out of hand. Smoke twisted lazily from the distant trees. She waited. Either it would disappear like a dream, the trees would burst into flames, or…

It continued to spiral upward.

"Am I dreaming? Is that smoke?" She pointed.

Josh jerked as if her words had pulled him from his lethargy. Sam leaned forward then jumped to her feet.

"It is smoke. I see it too." She bounced up and down. "Someone must live there."

Katie stood up and shaded her eyes to stare at the place. "How far is it, do you suppose?"

"Too far for me." Josh's weary voice indicated his level of fatigue. "You two leave me."

Sam and Katie both sat down beside him.

"I'm not going." Sam crossed her arms.

"I'm not leaving you." Katie wouldn't think of it. Except the only other option was to sit here and freeze… or starve. Which would come first? Which would be the more horrible?

She didn't voice her opinion for some time, trying to come up with a different solution. Finally, she had to speak.

"I'll head over there and get help."

Josh grabbed her arm. "It's too dangerous."

She patted his hand. "It's our best hope."

He pulled his hand away and formed two fists on his knees. "This is all my fault."

Katie turned to face him. He refused to meet her gaze. She removed her mitten and put a palm to his cheek, turning him toward her. Waited until he looked directly at her. She smiled and let him search her gaze, hoping… praying he would see her peace about their situation.

When the tension in his eyes faded, she spoke.

"Josh, I don't hold you responsible for anything except always taking care of us and encouraging us to trust God. Because of that, I believe God will guide us to safety. But—and this is equally important—if we perish, I will still trust God's love."

"Me too," Sam whispered, pressing her face to Josh's shoulder. "You're a good man."

Josh smiled. "Thank you both."

"Now let's prepare for what lies ahead."

"I'll go with you," Sam offered.

Katie reached over Josh to hug the girl. "I wish you

could, but I need you to stay with Josh and take care of him."

Sam nodded. "That makes sense."

"Let's get a camp made for you." Katie took the ax and returned to the trees to search for boughs for a bed. How long would it take her to go and get back with help? Sam gathered wood.

They soon had a fire going, water melting in the pot, and a bed made. Josh sat on the boughs but refused to lie down. "It's too late to start out today."

Katie nodded. "I know. It gives me time to leave things in place for you."

"I can take care of everything." Sam seemed a little miffed that Katie didn't realize it.

"I'll help you get more wood." The two of them went to the trees. Katie stopped. "Sam, I know how capable you are. But I don't know how long it will take to get to that place. You need to stick close to the fire and keep it burning. I didn't say anything, but I saw a mountain lion two days ago."

Sam's eyes widened. Then she lifted her chin. "I'll be careful, and I'll take good care of Josh." She looked back to where Josh sat by the fire. "Is there anything I can do for his leg?"

"I think it's quit bleeding since we stopped. I guess the best thing is to keep him from using it any more than he has to." That's why she'd set up camp close enough to the trees. He wouldn't have far to go to relieve himself.

They gathered wood until it was too dark to see then ate their almost depleted rations. She took a few pieces of dried meat, leaving some for the others.

"Time for bed," she said, when she'd done everything she could to prepare for her journey.

Sam and Josh lay down. Katie sat on a sack at the end of the bed, watching the fire.

After a few minutes, Josh eased to the end of the bed. "You have no idea how much I hate to see you doing this." His hand rested on her shoulder. "Please be careful. Who knows what sort of person you'll find at the cabin?"

His shudder vibrated on her shoulder.

She eased up to sit beside him. Behind them came Sam's gentle snore. The child slept peacefully. Might even do so after Katie left, leaving Josh to do things he shouldn't. It wasn't something she could control. It was in God's hands.

"Josh, you have taught us both to trust God. He will be with me and with you."

"I know. But there are men like Bull in the world."

"I promise I will be careful. I want you to promise me you will take care of that leg." There was so much more to say. "And yourself."

"I promise. Katie, if anything happens to either of us, I want you to know that I've learned to care deeply for you over these few days."

Her heart burst with joy at his confession. "And I for you."

They held hands and stared at the dancing flames. Although reluctant to end the moment, she knew he needed to rest, and she eased her hand free. "You sleep now."

But instead of returning to the bed, he put his arm around her and caught her chin with his other hand. His thumb rubbed along the bottom of her lip.

She gazed into his eyes. Drinking of the promises he offered. She saw his intention of kissing her and lifted her face.

His lips were cold. Firm. He moved his hand to cup her head. She leaned into him. This might be their first *and* final kiss, and she wanted to make it last for eternity.

She felt his lips curl into a smile and eased back enough to search his face.

He chuckled. "I think that's enough for tonight."

She drew her hand across his whiskered face, liking the soft feel of his beard. "Yes, you need to get some rest."

"You need to rest for your trip tomorrow." He squeezed her hand.

"I couldn't sleep for worrying about you."

After a bit, he shifted back to the bed. The fact convinced her how badly he was feeling.

Katie returned to watching the fire. Her pleasant memories would go with her down the hill to whatever she found in the trees.

If they got out of here alive, she would cherish that kiss for the rest of her life.

The next morning, they ate in silence. Katie used the time to drive determination into herself for the journey ahead. She reasoned the other two had thoughts of their time of waiting.

Josh's face was pale, as if he'd brushed it with a layer of snow. Katie wasn't sure it was from the pain in his leg —he'd leaned heavily on his cane as he went to the woods and collapsed on the bed as soon as he returned— or from his concern about her trip.

He pressed his hand to his wounded leg. "I'd give anything if you didn't have to go." A slow smile curved his mouth.

She realized she pressed her fingers to her lips, reminding them both of last night's kiss. Her cheeks burned as if she stood too close to the flames, and she turned away.

There was enough light for her to set out. She hugged Sam. "Keep the fire going."

"I will."

Josh stood, waiting, and Katie hugged him. He held her tight. "You be safe," he murmured.

"I'll do my best." She forced herself not to linger in his embrace.

She turned and began the descent. The snow was not as deep as higher up. She knew Sam and Josh watched her, but she resisted the urge to turn and wave until she had gone a goodly distance. They sat on the hill. They were too far for her to see their eyes or even the expressions on their faces, and yet she lingered a moment, burning the sight of them into her brain. *Lord, please bring us all safely back together.*

Her heart set on doing what she could to make that happen, she turned and continued onward. The trees were farther away than they appeared from up the hill. She dug a piece of dried meat from her sack and kept going as she chewed it. She plodded onward and onward. The hours dragged by on weary feet. The sun slowly dipped westward. Would she end up in the middle of nowhere and with nothing for the night? Josh had insisted she take one of the quilts and the flint, but there wasn't a tree in sight until she reached those she aimed for.

She washed another bite of meat down with a drink from the canteen and pushed onward. Her steps were flagging, and she gritted her teeth and forced herself to go faster.

She must reach the trees. She must get to the source of that smoke. She must get help.

She lost all sense of time and space. All that mattered was putting one foot in front of the other. She must get there. Get help. Rescue Josh and Sam.

With a start, she realized she could reach out and touch the trees. She glimpsed a candle flickering in a window. A bulky figure, not unlike Bull's build, passed the window.

Her heart stalled. Had he escaped and gotten ahead of them?

She sank to her knees as she tried to think what to do.

Josh had to remain calm, appear brave for Sam's sake. And his own. Panic would not serve any useful purpose. But as the hours of the afternoon dragged by, he'd watched Katie struggle through the snow, her steps growing slower and slower. She'd gone miles. The distance to the trees shrank so slowly he wondered if it was merely wishful thinking on his part. She was only a dot in the distance and then he couldn't see her. The sun lowered in the west. The light slanted through the trees covering the snow with dark shadows.

"She won't be back tonight." Sam sat beside him, her

hands rubbing restlessly on her thighs. "Maybe she won't be back at all." She burst to her feet and went beyond the fire to stare down the hill. "You shouldn't have let her go. Pa always warned me that many of the men living out here are no more tame than wild animals. He said they had no regard for how others should be treated. Especially women."

"That's not helping." He couldn't keep the weariness from his voice. It had been impossible to lose the tension gripping his neck. Indeed, it had grown worse with every passing hour. "I can imagine all sorts of horrible things without your help." Katie freezing to death in the woods. Maybe attacked by a wildcat. Even that might be preferable to falling victim to a crazy man.

Had he rescued her from one dreadful situation only for her to end up in a similar one? Or worse? The idea sent a spasm of pain through his entire being that made the pain in his leg pale in comparison.

He couldn't believe he'd rescued her, found her, only to lose her again.

He wouldn't believe it.

"Remember what she said? She would trust God. I will too. She'd want us both to."

Sam nodded then slowly turned away from study of the darkening hill and again sat beside him. "It's hard to trust when things all seem wrong."

He could think of no better way to comfort and strengthen them then to repeat some of the verses he'd learned. "'Mine enemies would daily swallow me up: for they be many that fight against me, O thou most High. What time I am afraid, I will trust in thee. I will not fear what flesh can do unto me.'"

Sam shifted so she could see his face. "You sure know a lot of verses. Guess that's because your pa was a preacher."

He chuckled softly. "I think my parents would have had us memorize scriptures even if Pa wasn't a preacher. They both felt knowing the verses by heart would guide us through life." He stared into the flames. "I think they'd like to know how much we appreciate the comfort they give even though they would be distressed by what we are going through."

He sank into silence. Realized how weary he was. His leg hurt something fierce. He'd glanced at it in the privacy of the trees. More than blood ran from the wound. Greenish pus did as well. No doubt it had been festering under the surface for months. Thanks to Bull's cruelty.

That wasn't what concerned him though. Not like the redness that stretched out from the wound.

"I think I'll sleep for a bit. Wake me if anything happens."

"Yeah." She sounded as weary as he felt. He promised himself he would rise during the night and make sure the fire was going.

The cold wakened him some time later. Or was it a sound? The fire was almost out. He scrambled from the bed, remembering too late about his leg. He bit back a cry and found the cane to lean on as he hobbled to the stack of wood and threw more on the embers, blowing on them to get the new wood burning.

When the flames licked upward, he looked for Sam. She was curled up in the remaining quilt, whimpering in her sleep.

He hopped to her side. "Sam. Wake up." He nudged her. "Wake up."

She jolted awake. Rubbed her eyes. "Katie? Is she..?"

"She went for help. Remember."

"I hoped she'd come back."

"Not yet." He had to give Sam hope that Katie would return. Had to give himself hope too.

"Sit beside me." He drew her to sit on the end of the bed. They could keep warm there, and his leg would be more comfortable.

He drew the fur around them, and they huddled together.

She soon slumped. Knowing she slept, he eased her back to the bed and pulled the fur around her. He added wood to the fire then curled up beside the girl in order to keep warm, vowing he would not sleep until he saw Katie again.

Dawn was a promise in the eastern sky when he slipped from bed, taking the quilt to wrap around his shoulders and leaving Sam huddled in the fur. He had been up several times to stoke the fire. *Katie, be safe. God, keep her in the palm of Your hand.*

He hobbled to where he could see the valley below, sat with the fire behind him and watched for light to creep into the hollows and illuminate the distant trees. Smoke trailed upward, filling his heart with hope.

Sam wakened and joined him. "See her yet?"

"Not yet." He offered her a piece of dry meat and ate one himself. Would not think how quickly they would run out of food if Katie didn't bring help. His leg hurt, but he pushed the pain aside. It was nothing compared to the ache in his heart as he thought of Katie.

Be safe. Be safe.

He sat on the cold ground to watch and wait.

Something flickered at the edge of the trees. He strained to make it out. Too big for one person. It moved smoothly. A mountain lion. But no, it grew in size and clarity.

"Is that a horse and sleigh?" His voice rang with wonder and gratitude that choked him so he couldn't continue.

"Yup." Sam laughed. "She's bringing help."

"Praise God. Praise God." His heart overflowed. How long would it take for the sleigh to cross the valley and climb the hill? It didn't matter. She was safe. They were all safe.

He pressed his hand to his leg. Now to get to a doctor and get this leg fixed before he lost it. He wished he could wait until he got back to Verdun and his ma's care, but he didn't think he better.

How long would it take for the infection to turn into blood poisoning?

atie leaned forward on the seat of the sleigh.

Skipper, who had welcomed her into his cabin last night and behaved like a gentleman, even going so far as to treat her like royalty, chuckled. "Can't make it go any faster that way."

He beamed at her. Several times he'd said how much he admired a young lady with spunk. "Hard to believe you hiked all that way. And alone. Mighty brave of you." He regarded her with such open approval that she squirmed in embarrassment. He was a youngish man though it was hard to guess his age. Likely close to Josh's age. He had deep brown eyes and reddish-brown hair tied back with a leather strap.

Although he'd asked several times how she and her companions came to be out in the middle of the mountains during the winter, she'd said she wouldn't tell him until they were all together. She couldn't say why she chose that answer, except it was their story, not just hers.

They were halfway across the valley. She squinted up the hill and made out the fire. "They must be okay. The fire is still burning."

It took another hour to get to the hill and climb it. The longest hour Katie had ever lived. She waved to Josh and Katie several times as they drew closer. Josh sat on the edge of the boughs. Sam jumped up and down and waved. Katie's gaze returned to Josh. Was he all right? All night she had worried his leg would get infected. As they got close enough that she could see their faces, she relaxed to see his smile.

As soon as they were close enough, she jumped down. Even before Skipper brought the sleigh to a halt. He reached out. "Careful, there, ma'am. Wouldn't want you injured."

She hugged Sam. "You're here."

Sam laughed. "Did you think we'd run away?"

Katie quirked her eyebrows as she drew Sam with her to Josh's side. "You're here. You're all right?"

He grabbed her hands. His smile filled her heart with sunshine warmth. "You made it. Thank God."

"Skipper, this is Josh and Sam. Skipper welcomed me into his home last night and was kind enough to come for you."

Skipper beamed at her praise. "Let's get you all back to my cabin. Get you warmed up. Maybe have a look at that leg."

Sam and Katie gathered up their few belongings, waving away Josh's help. "You get into the sleigh," Katie said.

The sleigh was a farm wagon that Skipper had put runners on for winter use.

"You sit on the bench with me." Skipper waved Katie forward as she prepared to climb in the back with Sam and Josh. Katie didn't want to offend the man, so allowed him to assist her to the seat.

"Now," he said, as they headed down the hill. "I would like to hear how you all came to be out here."

Katie still didn't know what to tell the man. If he was a friend of Bull's, what was to stop him from turning them all over to him? If indeed, Bull was still alive.

"Josh and I were lost and found Sam's cabin. We've been there since and still would be except the cabin burned down."

"Sam was alone? He's so young. Sam what's your other name?"

"Rimmer. I'm Sam Rimmer."

Skipper glanced over his shoulder. "You'd be Ike Rimmer's boy?"

Sam nodded. "He was my pa."

"I heard what happened to him. Sorry. I didn't know he had a boy, or I would have offered my help."

"I've done all right by myself."

Katie smiled at Sam's defensive tone.

Sam continued. "You want to help; you need to go to the sheriff and report Lambert Phillips for killing my pa."

"I surely would, except I didn't see him do it."

"Easy to say you would then, when you won't."

"Sam." Josh patted her arm. "There's nothing the sheriff can do unless a witness comes forward."

"Yeah, with Bull as a friend."

"You know Bull?" Skipper's face twisted in anger. "Now there's a man that deserves to hang."

Katie silently agreed.

"He's responsible for my brother's death."

"I'm sorry. But he may have paid for it." She told him about the avalanche. "I suppose there is a possibility that he survived." Her tone conveyed a healthy dose of doubt.

Skipper slapped his knee and laughed. "Justice may have been served."

Katie again silently agreed.

"So, after the cabin burned down, you decided to walk out?"

Josh answered. "Had no choice. We had very few supplies."

"How many days since you left?"

Katie couldn't rightly recall. "The days just seem to blend into each other."

"I believe this is the seventh day." Josh's voice was thin as if strained through a tight funnel.

The sun had passed its zenith by the time they reached Skipper's cabin. He took them inside. "I'll be right back. I have to take care of the horse."

The three of them stood in the middle of the floor. "It's even smaller than mine was," Sam said.

"We'll be a little crowded," Katie told her, "but soon we'll be in town."

"How far is it?" Josh asked, leaning heavily on his cane.

"I didn't ask. The only thing that mattered was getting back to you." Her cheeks burned at her boldness, but her heart ached with gratefulness for his safety and fear that their ordeal wasn't over yet. They still had to make it to town, and then Josh had to get help for his leg.

Skipper's boots thudded outside the door before he

stepped in. "Now find yourselves a place to perch while I make you something to eat."

Katie had enjoyed a hearty breakfast of cornbread and syrup. And a cup of hot tea, but the other two would be hungry as bears.

Skipper opened a little door by the stove and got a pot. "Stew," he said. "It keeps well out there. Might take a little time to thaw it out." He put it on the stove. Soon a tempting aroma wafted through the room.

Josh sat on the side of the bed, his face drawn and gray.

Katie was worried about him. "Josh, put your leg up."

"By all means." Skipper eyed the stained trousers. "I could look at it."

"I think it's best to leave it until we're in town."

"Whatever you think."

"How far to the nearest one?"

"That would be Glory. It's about three hours away, if the roads are good. I don't go often, but there's a preacher there. From what I've heard, he'll help you."

"Good to know."

"It's too late to start out today. Tomorrow we will go." Skipper stirred the stew. "Soon it will be warm enough to eat."

The man brought out an assortment of dishes. Two plates, two mismatched bowls. He held the second bowl a moment. "This was Kurt's special bowl. Kurt was my brother."

Katie could see nothing unusual about the bowl but knew when Skipper handed it to her that he had shown her his favor.

They all sat with food before them.

Skipper regarded them. "Is something wrong? Why don't you eat?"

"Josh usually prays before we eat," Sam said.

"Go ahead."

Josh's prayer was short but full of gratitude for safety and food and shelter. A sentiment Katie was sure they all shared.

Josh took a spoonful of the stew. "Skipper, this is the best food I've had in a long time. Thanks."

Skipper chuckled. "Best food in maybe seven days, if I'm right."

Josh laughed too.

Katie began to relax. They were safe. Tomorrow they would reach town. Then what? She didn't want to think about it.

She helped with the dishes, despite Skipper's protests.

The dishes done, he considered them. "There is time before bed for some entertainment." He rubbed his hands in glee.

Katie watched fear wreath Sam's face and caution draw Josh's mouth down. Like her, they wondered what form this entertainment would take.

Her concern mounted when Skipper reached under the bed. But then he drew out a funny looking thing consisting of a plaid sack and several horns.

Seeing the surprise of his audience, he explained. "My bagpipes. Have any of you heard them played?"

None of them had. Katie sat on the floor beside Sam. Josh lay semi-reclined on the bed.

Skipper filled the bag-like thing with air then began to blow and squeeze the bag at the same time. An earsplitting wail filled the cabin. The tune he played was sad enough to make the walls weep.

He stopped. "Nice, isn't it? Kurt used to do a reel to the music."

Katie did not dare offer an honest opinion. Nor did she venture to glance at Josh or Sam to see if they enjoyed it.

Skipper took their silence for approval and played again. And again. Until Katie feared her eardrums would explode.

She yawned hugely. Sam's head had fallen forward, though how the girl could sleep with that racket banging in her head was beyond Katie's understanding. She pointed toward the girl.

Skipper stopped. "I'm sorry. I know you all must be tired." He stowed the instrument under the bed again. "We're a wee bit short of beds. Katie, you sleep with your husband. That leaves me and young Sam to sleep on the floor."

"He's not my husband." The words blurted out before she could think better of saying them.

Skipper's brow furrowed. "Then..." He shook his head. "I don't understand. Why are you with him?"

Neither of them had said why they were alone in the wilderness.

"We were both lost." She could think of no other explanation.

"Well, that changes things." Skipper eyed Katie a long, uncomfortable moment. "I guess you don't want to share his bed?"

"That's correct."

"Then young Sam can. It was big enough for me and

Kurt, so it will hold the two of you." He again eyed Katie. "You'll be wanting some privacy, but I don't see how I can offer it."

"I'll sleep beside the bed on our fur rug. It's what we've been used to."

"Eh, but it's not fit for a lady." He continued to eye her openly to the point she backed up to the cot. When he'd thought her married, he had been a little too attentive. Now that he knew she was single; would his interest grow into annoying? Dangerous? Like those men back home that she had fled from.

Like Bull? She shuddered.

JOSH SETTLED into the most comfortable position he could find, but he would not rest easy. Not with Skipper watching Katie in such a predatory fashion. The man seemed decent enough, but he was still a man...and a lonely one, at that.

Katie lay on the fur, pressed as close to the bed as she could get. Josh didn't look at her but guessed if her eyes weren't open that she would, nevertheless, be tense, ready to jump up and flee.

Skipper grabbed a bedroll and lay on the floor as far from Josh and his entourage as possible, which, given the size of the room, was still within touching distance. He turned out the lamp and an uneasy darkness descended, filled with strange noises and uncertainty.

Sam curled next to Josh and was soon breathing deeply.

Josh was bone-weary, but he could not, would not,

relax. Not until they were in a place where he felt totally safe.

Where he could be certain Sam and Katie were safe.

He wakened to the lids of the stove rattling and jerked up to look around. His leg protested the sudden movement, but he managed not to groan.

Skipper was feeding the stove more wood.

Katie slept on the fur, her dark eyelashes forming a crescent against her cheeks. Her lips were slightly parted.

Josh remembered the taste of those lips. The coolness of them. He forced himself to turn away. He couldn't get out of bed without disturbing Katie, so he lay back again. He turned to Sam. Her blue eyes were wide as she watched Skipper. Then she brought her gaze to Josh and smiled. "Good morning, Josh."

"Good morning, Sam. I trust you slept well."

"Moderately so."

He chuckled. "You slept like a newborn baby."

"How do you know? You snored like a mad cow."

"A mad cow? Humph." But he laughed.

Katie sat up. "What are you two going on about?"

"Good morning," they said in unison.

Skipper called good morning to all of them. "Anyone want breakfast before we head out? Remember, it will take us at least three hours. But I understand if you are too anxious to eat before we leave."

Josh swung his legs over the side of the bed. By the tightness of his trouser leg he knew the wound had swollen. He couldn't get to town fast enough, but there was no need to leave hungry. "I doubt I will ever say no to the offer of food."

"Great. Then while you folks tend to your morning business, I'll bake biscuits to go with this porridge." He'd put a pot of ground oats on the back of the stove last night to simmer.

While the biscuits baked, Katie gathered up their belongings.

Josh offered to help but was secretly relieved when she said she could do it on her own. He was weary clear through to the point he could hardly stand upright. Thankfully, breakfast served to revive him.

"I'll get the sleigh when I've cleaned up the breakfast things," Skipper said.

"I'll do that." Katie waved him away.

It didn't take long for Katie to wash the dishes, nor for Skipper to bring the sleigh to the door.

Josh settled as comfortably as he could in the back, grateful for the fur robe. Sam sat beside him, wrapped in one of the quilts. Katie, again, sat up front beside Skipper. The man had tucked a robe around her knees. Patted it into place when Josh thought there was no need to do so.

He sat up and watched Skipper until they were on their way. The man had to spend a little of his attention on guiding the horse, so Josh slowly relaxed.

The trail was unbroken. The sleigh moved easily, but the horse broke through the crust of the snow and struggled forward.

Josh lay back. They would soon be in town. His nerves twanged like the ice on the lake they'd camped by.

He was counting on their situation to improve once

they reached Glory, but if Bull had lived and was still searching for them, or Phillips...

Town might not be as safe as he wished.

He fought sleep for a time, but he was tired. It had been days since he'd had a good night's sleep. Adding the injury to his leg on top of lack of sleep made it impossible to stay awake.

"Josh." He wakened to Sam shaking his shoulder. "I can see a town." She leaned over the side of the box to stare ahead.

He eased himself to the other side and turned so he could see. A big red barn dominated the scene. Snow-decked ground and winter-bare trees filled yards, but the most beautiful sight of all was the steepled church. It felt like he was coming home even though he knew it would take several more days of travel for him to reach Verdun.

He sat back. Did going to Verdun mean leaving Katie and Sam?

His heart almost tore as he considered his two options. Rejoin his family or make a new family with Katie and Sam. How he wished it was possible he could have both.

Of course, the answer to that did not lie solely with him.

Katie laughed at something Skipper said. They'd had all morning to get friendly, get to learn about each other. Maybe even decide there were things they liked about the other.

Josh admitted he and Katie had been thrust together —and not of her choosing. She had fought him in the beginning. Later, at Sam's cabin, they had become partners of sorts. But out of necessity more than choice.

Yes, she'd kissed him. Or rather, he'd kissed her. Perhaps the dire circumstances had influenced both of them.

He didn't dare assume what they had while running for their lives or trekking through the mountains or even sharing Sam's cabin was real. Katie might see him differently now that danger and necessity weren't factors.

He must be patient.

Never before had the word caused him such pain.

The wagon stopped. "I'll fetch the preacher." Skipper jumped down and strode to the door of the two-story house next to the church. There was a good-sized addition to the house. These people must have a large family. He grinned. Not unlike the Kinsley family.

Katie climbed down. Sam went to her side, and they waited for an invite into the house.

Josh edged toward the end of the wagon. He meant to be standing on his own two feet when the preacher saw him.

The door opened. A tall figure answered the door then stepped into the light.

Josh stared, sure his eyes had deceived him.

14

Katie saw the tall man with the kindly face, but before she could make his acquaintance, Josh gasped, and she spun around. "Josh, what's wrong?" His leg must be causing him so much pain he couldn't contain his groans. But he stared past her toward the man at Skipper's side.

"Pa?" Josh breathed the word.

Was he seeing things? Was he fevered? Lost in his mind?

"Pa." He shouted the word and took faltering steps forward.

The tall man rushed to Josh and wrapped his arms around him. "Josh, my son. My son. That which was lost is found. Praise God Almighty who has brought this to pass." He glanced over his shoulder. "Martha, come quick. He's here. He's returned home."

A woman rushed from the house. "What is it?"

Josh's pa stepped to Josh's side, his arm still around Josh's shoulders. "See for yourself."

The woman stared. Blinked as if she couldn't believe her eyes than rushed into Josh's arms, weeping profusely.

"It's all right, Ma. I'm back." Josh patted the woman. His pa wrapped his arms around them both and began to sing.

Praise God, from whom all blessings flow;
Praise Him, all creatures here below;
Praise Him above, ye heavenly host;
Praise Father, Son, and Holy Ghost. Amen.

Before he finished, Josh's mother had dried her eyes and joined him in song. Josh added a third voice.

Katie dashed away a few tears. She turned to Sam. Wonder and amazement filled the girl's face.

"Ma, Pa, I'd like you to meet Katie and Sam." Josh drew his parents toward them. "These are my parents, Martha Kinsley and Jacob Kinsley."

The couple welcomed them warmly.

Skipper cleared his throat. Josh chuckled. "I haven't forgotten you. Ma, Pa, this is Skipper, who rescued us and brought us safely here. He lives up in the mountains."

The man was greeted and thanked. Katie reached for their few belongings, but Mr. Kinsley took them. "Come on in, everyone. This calls for a celebration."

"I'm going to go home." Skipper turned his gaze to Katie. "Might be I'll come back to town in the near future."

Katie murmured something non-committal. She did not want to encourage his attention.

"If you come to a Sunday morning service, you're invited to have dinner with us afterwards," Mrs. Kinsley offered, which brought a wide smile to Skipper's face.

"I just might do that." He returned to his wagon, turning to wave as he drove from the yard.

"Now let's get you all into the house." Mrs. Kinsley bustled ahead of them. She eyed Josh as he stepped inside. "What is wrong with your leg?"

"I fell and injured it. Actually, injured an old wound." He sniffed. "Is that split pea soup I smell?"

His ma laughed. "It is indeed. I thought of you as I made it. Prayed for your safe return. And now here you are." She sniffed and dabbed at her eyes with her apron.

"And starving."

Katie tried to hide her amusement at Josh's words.

Mrs. Kinsley gave Katie a questioning look.

"He told us he would be hungry for a long, lo-o-o-o-ng time." She drew the word out.

Josh laughed. At least he appreciated her attempt at humor. "Ma, feed us, and we'll tell you about it."

"Sit down. All of you."

Katie sat with Sam as close as the chairs would allow. It was a long table, but they all sat at one end. Josh sat across from Katie, leaving a spot for his mother next to his father. Mrs. Kinsley set out bowls and filled them with steaming, thick soup. Then she sat down next to Josh and took his hand on one side and her husband's on the other.

"I'll pray," Mr. Kinsley said. He bowed his head. Cleared his throat several times before he could speak. His words were low, gravelly as he offered a heartfelt prayer of gratitude for his son's return and thanks for the food.

Over the meal, Josh told his parents why he hadn't contacted them for so long.

"You were held prisoner?" Mr. Kinsley was clearly shocked. "I'll speak to the sheriff. The man ought to be in prison for that."

"You might be too late, but at least the others could be released from their slavery," Josh said. "But I'm getting ahead of myself. First, I need to tell you how Katie and Sam became part of the picture." He told how Bull had bought Katie and how she and Josh had fled into the winter. "We were beyond hope when we smelled smoke and followed the scent to Sam's cabin. Sam had been alone since her father was murdered by Lambert Phillips —the same man who sold Katie."

"Oh, my dears." Mrs. Kinsley reached across and squeezed Katie's hands, but Sam put hers in her lap. Mrs. Kinsley's gaze went from Josh to Sam. "Did I hear you call Sam a she?"

Josh turned to Sam. His expression patient. "Sam?"

Katie could feel nervousness vibrating from the girl. "It's all right, Sam. Whatever you want to do."

Sam sucked in air then sat up straight. "My name is Samantha. Pa told me to pretend I was a boy. Said it was safer."

To her credit, Mrs. Kinsley showed no sign of shock. "I think your pa was a wise man."

Sam nodded. "I think so too."

The preacher turned the conversation back to Josh. "You waited a long time to try and escape."

Josh met Katie's eyes across the table. Their gazes held even as he talked. "I thank God that I was there to help Katie get away." He shifted his attention to his father, leaving Katie feeling she was falling through the air from a great distance. She hoped she would never land.

"I tried to escape twice before. The last time Bull shot me in the leg."

His mother gasped and his father looked thunderous.

"That's the wound I re-injured when I fell. But all it needs is Ma's special treatment." His grin was begging, teasing and loving all at the same time.

Katie wanted that sort of smile the rest of her life.

"We waited every day for a letter," his mother said.

"Ma, I'm sorry. I wrote once and then I kept putting it off because I didn't have anything special to say."

A moment of regret claimed Josh and his parents and then his ma pushed back from the table. "Josh, I'll have a look at that wound now."

"Ma, I'd love to let you, but first I would like to wash off many days of trail dirt, if you don't mind."

"Of course. What am I thinking? I'm sure you would all like baths."

Sam and Katie grinned at each other and nodded at her.

"I'll get you all different clothes too. As Josh knows, I keep a good supply of things for people like you who are in need of my help. Jacob, could you put water to heat for the baths?"

Her husband chuckled. "Have you forgotten I was heating water in the addition? I meant to give the place a good scrubbing." He stood. "That can wait. Come along, Josh. We'll get you cleaned up so your ma can see about that leg." Father and son went out the door.

"Excuse me," Mrs. Kinsley said. "I'll find some clothing." She hustled down the hall and into a room.

Sam and Katie looked at each other and laughed. "Can you imagine Josh finding his parents like this?"

"I know what he would say."

They laughed and spoke at the same time, saying, "God had it all planned." Then they laughed again.

"Let's do the dishes while the others are busy."

"You mean hovering over Josh?" Sam sounded so innocent, but Katie knew the girl's sly sense of humor.

"I guess they want to make up for lost time."

"Yeah, but he's a grown man."

At the wistful note in Sam's voice, Katie hugged her. "I don't think we ever outgrow the need and want for family."

Sam leaned into Katie. "What's going to happen to me?"

Katie eased her away so she could see the child's face. "I'm hoping you'll want to stay with me. We can make a family together."

"What about Josh? Can't he be part of our family?"

"If he wants to be." Things were different now. He was reunited with his parents. Perhaps that was all he needed.

"But we could ask him, couldn't we?"

Katie filled the dishpan as they talked and began to wash the dishes. She handed a bowl to Sam to dry. "I think we need to wait for him to say something first. After all, we don't want him to do it out of obligation."

Sam shrugged. "I wouldn't care why he did it so long as he says yes, he wants to stay with us."

"I'm afraid it's not that easy."

"Why not? Why can't we keep on the way we have been? I liked it."

"Me too. But a man and a woman don't just live together. It isn't right."

Sam stared at her. Then she nodded. "I know. You'd have to get married."

"That's right."

"How hard is it to get married? Does it cost a lot or something?"

"I think it's relatively easy and doesn't cost much."

"Then that's what you ought to do."

"Again, it isn't quite that simple. Both the man and the woman have to want it and agree to it."

Sam rocked her head back and forth. "Aren't you making it more complicated than it needs to be?"

"I don't think so. Here, dry the last dish. And just in time." Mrs. Kinsley returned, carrying an armload of clothing. She saw they had cleaned the kitchen.

"Why, thank you for helping." She picked a dress from the pile. A dark blue with white piping around the collar and down the front. "I think this might fit Sam. Or should I call you Samantha?"

"For me?" Sam's eyes were big and so blue Katie felt like she glanced into the brightest sky on the clearest day. "Oh." Sam fingered the material. "But it's so nice."

Mrs. Kinsley chuckled. "It's for you. You deserve it." She draped it over a chair.

Sam stared at it, swallowed hard. "You can call me Samantha." Her face wrinkled up. She blinked several times and rubbed at her nose. Thankfully, Mrs. Kinsley ignored it and held out a fawn-colored dress with a darker brown bodice. "Katie, I think this will fit you."

"It's lovely. Thank you." Her dress was torn and muddy.

Mrs. Kinsley set out two other piles. "Unmention-ables for you both."

Poor Sam blushed to the roots of her hair.

"I have trousers and a shirt and whatnot for Josh. I'll take it out to him and see to his leg at the same time." She bustled out the door and into the addition.

Sam and Katie grinned at each other then watched out the window.

"I wish I could see what's going on," Sam murmured.

"Me too. But maybe we can hear." Katie cracked the window open. A blast of cold air rushed in, but they both kept their ear to the opening.

At first, they heard only murmuring, the rattle of a kettle, and then silence.

Katie whispered to Sam. "I expect she's examining his wound. Maybe cleaning it up."

"I hope it's all right."

Katie squeezed Sam's hand. "Me too." After a few minutes of silence, she said, "I'm getting cold. I'm going to close the window."

But Josh's voice came to them, and she changed her mind.

His words were firm. Almost defiant. "Ma, I am not going to stay in bed. I will rest my leg, but only if I can sit up in the kitchen with everyone else."

The murmur of other voices reached them, but they couldn't make out the words.

Sam and Katie grinned at each other. "Maybe he wasn't so stubborn when they last saw him," Sam said.

"He learned that when he had to deal with Bull."

"And when he led us off the mountain."

Katie nodded. "And when he decided to keep going even after he hurt his leg again."

"Do you think they'll listen to him?" Sam put her ear back to the opening.

Katie chuckled softly, her mind flooding with all sorts of memories. Of Josh keeping her warm in the woods against all odds. Of his determination to keep going until they reached help. Of his careful planning for leaving in the spring. And how he'd made sure they were safe on the journey out.

"I think if they don't, they'll find he is like those mountains and will not be moved."

Sam straightened and faced her. "I like thinking of him that way. Solid and unmovable as the Rocky Mountains."

"They're coming. He's limping beside his Pa." Katie quietly closed the window, and they moved away from it to watch the door.

Mrs. Kinsley came in first, shaking her head. "I'd forgotten what a stubborn person he is. Either that, or he's a lot more stubborn than he used to be."

"Maybe he's had to be in order to survive the last year."

Mrs. Kinsley smiled at Katie. "Thank you for reminding me that it's a good thing." She turned to Josh who had entered leaning on his Pa's arm. "Now you promised to sit with your leg up. Will the rocking chair do?"

"It will be fine, Ma." He sank into it, and she placed a stool under his foot.

Sam stared at Josh. "You look pretty good all slicked up."

"I know." Josh pretended to preen. Then his gaze slid to Katie, and his smile tipped sideways.

She couldn't decide whether to shake her head or nod. To smile or cry. The black shirt his mother had given him made his eyes more gray than blue. He had shaved, revealing the fine shape of his chin. She could more clearly see his lips.

Her tongue refused to work, which was just as well, for she feared she could not find an intelligent word to speak.

His smile lingered in his eyes. "Ma insisted on these baggy trousers so she could tend my wound."

That snapped Katie from her stunned state. "What about the wound? How bad is it?"

"Ma drained pus from it and put on some nasty smelling ointment that she says will draw out the poison and ease the pain."

"Has it? Eased the pain, I mean?"

"I believe it has."

If Mrs. Kinsley hadn't spoken right then, Katie wondered how long the two of them would have stood with their gazes locked. "I've seen worse and seen them heal." Doubt and concern filled her voice. "We'll have to wait and see how this does. Of course, it would help if you rest it."

Josh patted the arms of the wooden rocker. "This *is* resting."

Mr. Kinsley cleared his throat, perhaps hoping to forestall an argument between his son and his wife. "I'll empty out his bath water and prepare one for your ladies. Which of you wants to go first?"

Katie couldn't wait to get out of her clothes and get

clean all over. But she wanted to help Sam. If Sam would let her.

"Sam, you can go first, then I can linger as long as I like." That left little room for the girl to argue.

A few minutes later they both went to the addition, each carrying a stack of clothing. The place was warm. The tub sat full of hot water. Katie glanced into the other doorways. There were two rooms, each with two beds.

"They're for sick, injured, and people needing shelter," the preacher said. "Not often are they empty. My wife sent this along." He handed them a bar of scented soap.

Katie held it to her nose and breathed in rosewater scent. She held it out to Sam to smell.

"Nice," Sam said.

Katie guessed the girl would enjoy all kinds of girlie things given the chance, and she meant to give her the chance.

"Throw your old clothes into that basket," the preacher said. "My wife will see if anything can be salvaged. I'll leave you two to do what you need to do. No need to rush back in. Take your time."

As soon as he left, Sam began to strip her clothes off, tossing each item into the basket. "I hope I never again have to wear baggy shirts and pants."

"Into the water and scrub, scrub, scrub. Call me when you're done, and I'll wash your hair for you. I'll be in one of the bedrooms." The girl needed her privacy.

Sam needed no more urging.

As Katie waited in the other room, she listened to Sam singing as she washed. It pleasured Katie to hear the girl enjoying her bath.

"Done," Sam called a little later.

Katie scrubbed Sam's hair and then helped her get into the various items of clothes. "Sit down and I'll do your hair." It had enough length to pin back and, as it dried, the ends curled. "Let me have a look at you." The girl pirouetted. "Sam, you are beautiful. I think I will have to start calling you Samantha."

"Do you think Josh will think I'm pretty?"

"He will unless he's blind."

Samantha giggled.

"I'll go with you into the house while Josh's pa gets water ready for me." She thanked Mr. Kinsley for preparing her bath water.

"Not at all, my dear. We love helping others, and to know you have shared part of Josh's life makes you special in our eyes."

Katie choked back tears and hurried into the house with Sam. She held back, letting the girl go ahead.

Josh stared. "Sam? You're not a boy any longer. You're a beautiful young lady."

Sam colored up. "I know."

"I think I will be beating the young men off with a stick."

Sam's eyes widened, and she shook her head hard enough Katie feared the combs would go flying. "No, you won't. I don't care for young men."

Josh's grin slowly faded. "How many do you know?"

Sam tossed her head. "None."

Josh chuckled. "I predict that will soon change."

Mr. Kinsley returned to say Katie's bathwater was ready.

Katie hurried away with Josh's chuckles ringing in her ears.

She meant to soak away the dirt of the trail, but also every worry about what direction her life would take next.

Knowing Josh would tell her that she could trust God with the future, she tried to do that.

But what was going to happen to them now?

JOSH HAD SO MANY QUESTIONS. "How did you end up here of all places?"

His pa said they had moved in the hopes of locating him. "I believe God led us here, and having you delivered to our doorstep confirms it."

"Where are the girls?" He soon learned they were all married and lived nearby.

"Even Adele? When I left she was married to Floyd."

His parents told him that Floyd had died, and Adele had a young son named after his grandfather. He wanted to hear everything about his sisters, but he kept listening and watching for Katie to return.

When she stepped into the room, wearing a fetching dress, her face glowing from the scrubbing and her damp hair hanging loose down her back, he forgot to breathe.

He'd considered her attractive before, but she was stunning now. He tried not to stare but couldn't seem to drag his gaze away from her.

Her cheeks colored up like a sunrise sky.

Sam laughed. "Josh, you seem surprised."

He swallowed and tore his gaze away. "Nah. Just glad to see you both looking and smelling better."

Sam gave him a playful slap on his shoulder. "Applies to you too, you know."

He knew. They were all different here.

He could hardly expect things could continue as they had. He must allow Katie time to adjust to this life.

Patience, Josh, he warned himself.

But there wasn't enough patience in the whole world to make him willing to wait. Willing even, to let her pursue a path that didn't include him.

15

_____

Over the next few days, Josh learned he had to be patient in many areas. Sitting idle soon lost any charm he ever thought it might have even though his parents, Katie, and Sam all did their best to keep him amused.

He enjoyed their company. Especially Katie and Sam's. It was so much like the closeness they had shared while at Sam's cabin. Besides, they made him laugh. He especially enjoyed it when Katie leaned close enough that he could breathe in the smell of roses. Her hair tickled his chin, triggering a desire to stroke it. He stuffed back the longings. They were no longer in any danger.

They were in the midst of a checker tournament when Ma hurried into the room.

"You have a letter. It came for you when we were still in Verdun. I'd completely forgotten it until I sat at my desk a minute ago."

He took the rumpled envelope and glanced at the postmark before he broke the seal. "It was mailed in

Verdun." He took out the page and glanced down to the signature. "It's from Eliza. Probably to inform me of her marriage." Though why would she think he wanted to hear that news? He scanned the letter. "She didn't get married. Wonders if I would care to call on her." He crumpled the page and threw it at the ash pail. Did she think he was fool enough to trust her again?

But the letter served to remind him of what she'd said the last time he saw her. She'd told him his prospects were lacking.

What would she say now? He had even less.

Katie had disappeared after he read the letter. But he and Samantha continued to play checkers.

Day after day passed as he waited for his leg to heal.

Sunday came and went. Ma insisted he remain at home. The weather was cold and stormy, so attendance at church was low. Ma and Pa had decided not to let his sisters know he was home for fear they would try and travel in the bad weather. He longed so badly to see them that his insides felt hollowed out.

Resting his leg might have been bearable if it showed any improvement.

Ma did her best to be encouraging, but she couldn't completely hide her concern. She tried compresses. She applied various ointments she had made.

"It will take time." Her words seemed more like a warning than encouragement.

"I know it's not healing."

She nodded. "The redness isn't as bad. That's a good sign." She met his eyes and seemed to see his need to know what he would deal with in the future. "I'm doing my best and praying for it to heal, but I'll be honest with you. I think this leg will likely bother you the rest of your life."

He jerked forward, ignoring the pain the movement sent shuddering up his leg. "You mean I'll be crippled?"

"You might always limp." She gave a chuckle that lacked amusement. "But you'll be able to forecast the weather."

He fell back, his head tipped to the wooden bars of the chair.

"I'm grateful you're alive. You should be too." His mother tidied up the things from cleaning his wound and went down the hall.

Katie and Sam had been in the parlor while Josh had his leg tended, and they returned to the kitchen. He guessed from the way their mouths smiled but their eyes held hurt that Ma had told them her verdict.

He did not want their pity.

Sam brought out the checkerboard. "I'll play you the best out of three."

Normally he would have asked what the winner would get, but he shook his head. "I don't feel up to a game right now."

"Okay. I have other things I can do." She put on her coat and left the house.

"She'll go see your pa's horse."

Josh knew Katie meant to be encouraging...or something.

He could not look at her. She deserved far better than a penniless, crippled man. "I'm going to bed." He grabbed his cane, pushed past Katie, and went to the bedroom across the hall from his parents' room where he'd been sleeping.

Here he was, twenty-six years old, living at home, living off his parents' generosity.

He lay staring at the ceiling while pots and pans rattled in the kitchen.

Sam and Katie's voices came to him. They laughed.

He groaned. He wanted to be with them. To make a home with them. But they deserved so much better.

Lying on the bed wishing things could be different wasn't helping him feel better, so he sat up. Ma had placed a Bible on the table by his bed. *God, I need Your help and guidance. Speak to me.* He opened the Bible randomly, hoping for something to help.

It was the book of Esther. He knew the story. How Esther was chosen to be the queen. How an edict against the Jews had been issued, and she was the only one who could speak to the king. It might cost her her life to do so, but her cousin said...Josh searched for the exact words. "Who knoweth whether thou are come to the kingdom for such a time as this?"

Thank you, Lord.

Peace and pain mingled in his heart. If he had only been brought into Katie and Sam's lives to help them get off the mountain, he would rejoice at having done so. And if that was the end of their lives being intertwined, well, he would say with Esther, 'If I perish, I perish." He could even smile about how dramatic his thoughts were. After all, he wouldn't die.

At least not literally. He would learn to deal with the pain in his heart just as he must learn to deal with the pain in his leg.

He rejoined the others. He played checkers with Sam.

He laughed and talked and congratulated himself that no one knew how much effort it took.

BUT THE NEXT morning when Pa announced he was going to ride south to check on a few people, Josh made up his mind.

"I'll go with you, Pa. I'm getting cabin fever."

Katie and Sam looked at each other in mock horror, making him laugh as they shared a sweet memory.

His ma began to protest.

"Ma, I've made up my mind."

"You need to rest your leg."

"I have been. Has it done any good?"

"You have to be patient."

"I've about used up all my patience. I'm sorry, Ma, but I'm going." He met Katie's gaze, saw the worry in Sam's face. "I'm sorry," he murmured.

"You're welcome to come with me," his pa said. "I'd like your company. Let me get a horse from Mickey at the livery."

And if Josh needed any more indication of his sad state of affairs, this was it. He didn't even have his own horse.

A little later he and Pa were on their way. Josh had little to say, but he did lots of listening. Pa pointed out familiar places. "Stella and Bruce live there."

"Do I know them?"

Pa chuckled. "You don't." He told about a woman and her two children being rescued by Flora and her husband. "Of course, they weren't married then. That's quite a story."

Pa told about Flora being stranded in a snowstorm. And how, when Pa insisted they must marry after spending two nights together, Kade had asked for time to win her over. "And he did."

Josh laughed. A sincere laugh. "Where do they live?" He couldn't wait to see them and knew they would be as eager to see him.

"We'll stop on the way back if it isn't too late." After a bit, Pa turned to the left. "We're going to visit an old friend, Stewart Kennedy. He's alone and a bit crusty. But he's always eager for a visit."

They rode onward. Cows and horses grazed where the snow left the ground bare. Josh glanced around. If he had money or a chance to follow his dream, he'd get land around here and start ranching. If he was to enjoy the whole dream, he would add Katie and Sam to the picture.

His dreams were but empty wishes.

"This is the place."

A little house was tucked into a background of trees with a hill rising behind it. Josh turned in his saddle. The cabin faced the mountains. The view reminded him of the scene he had shared so many times with Katie and Sam. If he could afford a place, he'd want one like this.

A gray-whiskered man called to them from the open door. "Thought you might decide to stay close to town for the winter," he said to Pa as they went inside.

The house was a comfortable size. Bigger than Sam's cabin had been. In fact, Josh wondered if the man once had a family or wished for one.

He gave the place closer study. A roomy kitchen with a cozy sitting area on the other side. He leaned forward to peer out the window by the armchair. It allowed a nice view of the mountains. Two doors opened off the sitting area. The door to one was ajar, and he glimpsed an unmade bed and a messy room. It was a large place for one old man.

Pa introduced Josh to Stewart.

Stewart eyed him up and down. "So, this is the missing prodigal son. Boy, why didn't you write?"

Josh told his story. He was careful to inform the older man that he'd written a letter that for some reason hadn't been delivered.

Stewart nodded as Josh spoke, and then asked a few questions. "Your pa never stopped believing he'd find you."

"I never gave up praying I'd get away."

"What are your plans now?" Stewart asked.

"I need a job. I need to learn everything I can about ranching because one day I'd like to have my own ranch."

"A noble goal."

Talk turned to other things. After an hour of visiting, Pa prayed with the man, and they departed. On their horses again, Pa glanced at the sky. "I think we have time to visit Adele and Ethan."

"I'd like that."

They arrived in time for dinner. Pa knocked at the door then stood aside as it opened. Adele stared at Josh. Her mouth opened but nothing came out. Then she threw herself into his arms, sobbing. He chuckled and patted her back.

"Nice to see you too, Adele."

Adele dried her eyes. She patted Josh's cheeks. "Is it really you? How I've prayed for this day." She hugged him again then introduced her husband, young Jake, plus Jake's new brother, Georgie, and sister, Susie.

They sat down at the table. Adele kept looking at Josh and sniffing. They could have spent hours catching up on all the news, but Pa said they had to be on their way. Adele hugged Josh tight. "I am so glad you are back safe and sound."

"Me too."

They rode back toward town. Pa turned into the lane leading to Flora's place. Josh's throat tightened. He couldn't wait to see the little sister who had caused him the most grief.

She stood in the doorway watching the riders' approach. Shaded her eyes and squinted at Josh, trying to identify him.

He knew the minute she did. She raced across the yard, unmindful of the cold and the snow. "Josh!" she screamed. She grabbed his leg. Thankfully it was his good one. "Josh, you're back." Tears streamed down her face.

"Let go of me so I can get down."

She stepped back. "Hurry up."

His feet barely touched the ground before she threw herself into his arms, laughing, crying, and screaming. "You are never to disappear again. You hear me?"

"I don't know. I think I might be deaf in this ear from all your screaming."

A tall man strode from the barn. He gave Josh a hard look. "You better have a good reason for holding my wife like that."

Flora grabbed one of the man's hands. "It's Josh. Josh, this is my husband, Kade."

"Pleased to meet you." They shook hands. "Maybe not as glad as she is."

Flora practically hung from Josh's arm.

Josh laughed. "She always was a clinger."

"Was not." She gave his arm a playful swat. "Come on in. I warn you, you better have a good explanation for where you've been hiding." They walked toward the house. She stopped. "You're limping. Why?"

His leg hurt something fierce. Ma was right to say he needed to rest it, but he didn't regret not listening to her. Seeing two of his sisters went a long way to healing a different pain—the one in his heart at the knowledge of his inadequacies.

They were deep into catching up when Pa spoke. "We need to get back, so your ma won't worry."

"You can't leave yet," Flora protested. "We've got so much to talk about." She brightened. "Josh, why don't you stay? We can put you up for a few days or however long you want to be with us."

Kade added his welcome to the invitation. "That's a great idea."

Pa seemed troubled. "What about your leg? Ma will want to be tending it."

Flora waved away his protest. "I can take care of it."

Pa shook his head. "Your ma won't be happy with me."

"You simply have to smile and kiss her, and she'll forgive you anything."

They all laughed at Flora's airy words.

With that assurance, Pa left.

❧

WHEN MR. KINSLEY arrived back home with the announcement that Josh meant to stay with Flora, Katie knew she hadn't been imagining the growing distance between herself and Josh. She'd thought he cared about her. And Samantha. But it appeared he was like those men back home who pretended an interest in her with no desire for commitment.

Or perhaps he planned to return to Verdun. And Eliza.

Whatever his plans, he'd not indicated in any way that he meant for her or Samantha to be part of them.

It was time to move on. They couldn't continue to live off the charity of his parents. Nothing called her back east. Besides, Samantha was a child of the west. Despite looking pretty in dresses and enjoying having her hair done, Sam would always be a little wild.

Thankfully, she had the money to live on her own. She and Samantha.

She'd spoken to Mr. White at the store about buying or renting a home, and he'd arranged for her to see one. They were going there today.

She and Samantha walked down the street toward the place.

"Why are we doing this?" Sam asked, her voice sharp with disapproval.

"We need to move on with our lives."

"But not without Josh." The girl could be as stubborn as Josh when she put her mind to it.

"Samantha, it's like I told you. A person has to *want* to be with another person. You can't force two people together."

"What did you do to make him not want to be with you?"

"Nothing that I can think of."

"Then what did you do to make him know you want to be with him?"

Katie's steps slowed. What had she done? Besides sit up all night to keep him safe? Besides hold tight to him when they faced cold weather, fires, being lost? Besides kissing him? "He ought to know how I feel."

Samantha snorted. "I remember something my pa used to say when I told him things like that."

Katie stopped and waited for the girl to tell her.

"He said it wasn't fair to be judged for something I hadn't told him. Said he wasn't a mind reader." She sniffed. "I don't think Josh is a mind reader either."

"No, I'm sure he's not." But she could hardly blurt out to Josh that she loved him and hoped they could be a family.

Mr. White waited on the doorstep for them. He greeted her and told her all the fine points of the house as he let her in. Katie went through the rooms. She could see the possibilities of it becoming a home.

But a home needed a family. She and Samantha were a family.

The house was nice. But it wasn't right. Nothing about the situation was right.

Samantha raced through the rooms. She went to each window. "You can't see the mountains." She leaned against a wall, no longer interested.

Katie could not see herself here. "I'm sorry," she told Mr. White. "But I'm not ready to make this decision."

"It's not a problem. The house isn't going anywhere. You know where to find me if you change your mind."

"Thank you."

"Now what?" Samantha demanded when the man had left.

"I don't know. Let's walk for a bit." Her thoughts tumbled and turned. It seemed that what she wanted she couldn't have. Could she settle for second best without trying hard for best?

They wandered by the livery barn. Mickey, the owner, whom she'd met twice, came out, leading a fine-looking horse. She stopped to watch.

"You like this horse?" he asked.

"I don't know much about them, but he appears to be a good horse."

"The best. I bought him from a rancher. I figure I can sell him easily enough."

"How much?"

Mickey named a sum. It seemed reasonable to Katie.

"How much with all the tack?"

She barely waited for Mickey to give the amount. "I'll buy it. I'll be back with the money." She hurried toward the manse.

"Why are you buying a horse?" Samantha asked.

"It's not for me."

"Oh." A beat of silence. "It's for Josh, isn't it?"

"Yes. You think he'll like it?"

"If he doesn't, he needs his head examined."

They slipped into the manse and up the stairs to the room they'd been sharing. Katie knew there were scissors in the cupboard and got them. She carefully picked out threads inside the lining of her coat.

"What are you doing?" Samantha demanded.

"Getting the money for the horse." She withdrew several bills.

"You're carrying around a bunch of money?"

"I had a house back in Missouri. Brought the money with me. Knew I'd need it sooner or later."

They returned to the livery barn with the money, and she made arrangements for the horse to stay there until Josh returned. Mickey agreed to take it to the pen behind the manse when he saw Josh come home.

Now all they had to do was wait for him to come back.

This was his last chance. When she gave him the gift, his reaction would make it clear if there was any hope for them.

She didn't have long to wait. He returned that afternoon.

His ma fussed over him and insisted on checking on his wound.

Several times Josh glanced at Katie in a way that made her think he had something he wanted to say to her.

He'd get his chance. As soon as his parents had had their say, she asked Josh to go outside with her. "I have something to show you." Mickey had led the horse to the barn shortly after he saw that Josh had returned home. "If your leg is up to it."

"My leg is fine." He set his jaw as if to inform one and all that he would not let it bother him.

They left the house. She knew Samantha would watch from the window.

They went to the pasture.

He studied the horse for a moment. "Whose horse is that?"

"It's yours."

He stared at her. "What are you talking about?"

"It's my gift to you."

"Why? And where did you get money for an animal like this?"

"I have money from the sale of my house. As to why, I wanted you to know how I feel about you."

He stepped away from the fence and stared at her, his eyes dark with an emotion she couldn't understand.

"You see me as a helpless crippled man who has to depend on someone else? I won't depend on your money or your charity." He strode away from her as fast as he could go.

She watched through a curtain of tears.

She didn't see him as crippled or helpless.

Quite the opposite. He was a man she knew she could depend on.

JOSH WENT inside the church and plunked down on a pew. Katie had money. He had nothing. Nothing at all to offer a beautiful woman like her.

Pa came in and sat beside him. "Son, I was in the barn. I couldn't help but overhear you and Katie."

Josh shrugged.

Pa continued. "Why do you think Katie bought that horse for you?"

"Because I can't buy my own."

"I think you could find work and buy a horse, if that's what you wanted."

Josh shrugged again.

"Son, what's really going on here?"

"Isn't it obvious? I have nothing to offer someone like Katie. I have no money, no prospects, and I will likely be a cripple the rest of my life." Ma had only said he'd have a limp, but it felt like cripple to him.

"Josh, you're letting circumstances direct your thoughts and your life. I taught you better than that."

Josh didn't say anything.

"If we only trust God when things are going the way we think they should, then we aren't truly trusting God."

"Pa, I thought I learned that lesson while I was held captive and forced to work in that mine. But that seems so trivial compared to this. I love Katie, but I have nothing to offer her."

Pa squeezed Josh's shoulder. "There is no better gift than love. Find that girl and tell her how you feel."

"I'm afraid she'll see me as having no prospects."

Pa was silent a moment. "You know, that seems more like something Eliza would say than something Katie would."

It was true. Josh laughed. "I'm going to find Katie."

Ignoring the way his leg protested, he hurried into the house. He glanced around the kitchen. Sam and Ma were working on a meal. "Where's Katie?"

Sam scowled at him. He hoped he could soon turn that into a smile.

"She went out," Ma said. "Said she had to see about a house."

"A house? What does that mean?"

Sam rose to her feet and with fists clenched, spat out her words. "She's going to buy a house for me and her. All because you don't love her."

"But I do."

Sam's anger gave way to shock, and then she grinned. "Why don't you tell her that?"

"Where is she?"

"I'll show you." She grabbed her coat.

They made their way down the street.

"I'd like to tell her by myself."

Sam grinned. "I'll make myself scarce."

"Good girl."

"That's the house." She pointed. "Now be sure you tell her."

"I will."

He opened the door without knocking. "Katie?" She stood in the middle of the empty room; her face wet with tears. "Oh, Katie. Forgive me." He held his arms out to her.

She shook her head.

He lowered his arms. "Katie, I've been staying away from you because you deserve so much more than a man with no money who might have a bum leg the rest of his life. I'm not much of a prize."

She scrubbed the tears from her face. "You're the only prize I want."

"You really mean that?" He closed the distance between them. They stood inches from each other but not touching. "Katie, you are the bravest, strongest woman I know. And the most beautiful. I was afraid what we had up in the mountains would go away when we were finally safe. But for me it hasn't."

She pressed her palms to his cheeks. "Being with you makes me feel whole."

He lifted her chin. "Katie, I love you. I'd like to marry you, if you are agreeable."

She nodded. "I love you. I will gladly marry you. I see us having a lovely future together."

He cupped his hands to her head and kissed her. It was everything he remembered and so much more. It was promise for the future.

"About time." They broke apart at Sam's words. "Guess that means you'll keep the horse."

"It does. Thank you for thinking of me." His smile at Katie was returned with such joy that he almost forgot Sam watched them. He held out an arm. "Come here, girl."

She came.

"How would you like to be part of our family?"

"Yes. Yes. Besides, I don't think you could get along without me."

Katie and Josh laughed and hugged the girl.

"I don't think we could." He kissed the top of Sam's head, and when Katie lifted her face to him, he kissed her again.

EPILOGUE

*C*hristmas Day
Katie vibrated with excitement. She and Josh had planned a surprise for his family. Only his parents and Samantha knew what they were going to do.

When Josh learned that all his sisters and three other couples who were almost family were to be there for Christmas, he said he wanted to be married in front of his entire family.

They'd planned the event carefully, not wanting to steal from any of the Christmas festivities.

One by one, the family members arrived. When the girls saw Josh, they flung themselves into his arms, crying and screaming.

Josh met his brothers-in-law and new nieces and nephews. For Katie and Sam everyone was new though Mrs. Kinsley had been preparing them for their first encounter.

"This is Flora and Kade." Josh introduced them. Katie knew how they had met.

He introduced Victoria and Reese. Katie still found it hard to believe that Victoria had lost her memory four years ago. How strange that would be.

Josh drew her and Samantha onward. "Hi Eve. I see you and Cole are together forever." Josh introduced Cole's mother and aunt. And they both met young Matt for the first time.

They moved on to meet and greet Josie and Walker.

Josh had previously met Adele's husband Ethan and their three adorable children, Jake, Georgie and Susie.

Katie's head was beginning to hurt from trying to keep everyone straight as Josh's ma introduced Stella. "She lived with us a number of months. This is her husband, Bruce and his Aunt Mary." They met the two children, Blossom and Donnie.

Katie had started mumbling names under her breath. Josh leaned down and whispered in her ear. "We have years and years to sort them all out."

She was convinced she would need that long as Josh's mother led her to another couple. "Clara and the young preacher, Alex." They had a little boy of about four.

The introductions continued. Only Josh didn't wait for his ma to introduce the next couple. "Tilly." He hugged her off the floor.

Katie's eyes clouded with tears to see his joy at meeting this sister. When Josh released her, Tilly introduced her husband, "Lance, and our two daughters, Valerie and Emily."

Their love for each other was so evident it made them glow.

There was Hunter and Dottie and a six-year-old boy named Rusty.

The food was almost ready when Katie and Samantha slipped upstairs and changed into the gowns they had chosen for the event. Katie had once dreamed of a frothy white dress and walking down the aisle on her father's arm. But in the end, none of that mattered. All she wanted was to join her life to Josh's. So, she had chosen a pale brown dress in a simple style that she could wear often in the future. She'd purchased the fabric and sewn the dress herself.

She'd let Samantha chose the material for her dress, and the girl had picked out a royal blue sateen and chosen a simple style. Katie had helped her sew the gown.

As soon as Samantha was in her dress, Katie did her hair. It was something she did for Samantha that they both enjoyed. The girl's hair had grown out some, and Katie brushed it back, letting it hang down the girl's back. She gave Samantha the gift she'd purchased for her —a pair of beautiful combs to hold her hair back.

"We're ready." She'd earlier done her own hair in a simple braid coiled around her head.

Katie signaled at the top of the stairs where Mrs. Kinsley waited, then backed out of sight.

Her future mother-in-law called for quiet. "If you could all crowd into the parlor." They had shoved the furniture to the edges of the room.

The family made their way into the sitting room. Everyone talked at once. Such a contrast to the quiet family gatherings she'd enjoyed as a child.

She and Josh had discussed family. They both wanted as many children as God saw fit to bless them with. They had discussed another matter as well. He had informed her recently that the sheriff had gone to investigate the crimes committed by Lambert Phillips and Bull. It turned out that Bull had indeed disappeared the day of the avalanche. And Lambert had been shot by someone faster and smarter who didn't take kindly to being cheated.

"Justice has been served," Josh had said.

"And your leg is finally healing," she'd pointed out. "It reminds me of your story about bad bringing something good."

He'd given her a teasing smile. "What good do you mean?"

She stroked his dear face. "You and me and Samantha. What could be better?"

"We're ready," Mrs. Kinsley called, drawing Katie from her musings.

Samantha went down the stairs first and paused at the doorway. As they had discussed, Josh would be on the other side of the door.

It was all Katie could do not to rush down the stairs and into his arms. Instead, she descended slowly, and regally, she hoped. She turned the corner into the room. Josh waited, smiling. He'd recently had his hair cut. He was clean shaven. And looked so good. So kissable.

She felt her cheeks warm and told herself to keep her thoughts under control.

Josh crooked his arm toward her, and she took it. She and Samantha clasped their hands on the other side, and the three of them stepped forward to where Josh's father waited.

Suddenly, one or two of his sisters realized what was going on.

"They're getting married," Flora yelled.

A roar of cheers and clapping greeted the announcement.

They spoke their vows.

"I now pronounce you man and wife. You may kiss your bride."

Josh kissed her thoroughly. Her cheeks burned when he finally lifted his head. They pulled Samantha to them.

His family surrounded them, congratulating them.

The rest of the day passed in a blur. They ate a sumptuous dinner, and no one seemed to mind how crowded they were.

They opened gifts. She'd made tea towels for Josh's mother and embroidered a bookmark for his father.

For Samantha, she'd chosen a new brush set. Sam was pleased.

She handed Josh his gift. It was an embroidered hanging to go in their new home. *In God We Trust.*

He gave her a large key that was actually their names intertwined. "The key to my heart," he whispered.

"Big heart," she whispered back.

He grinned. "Getting bigger every day, thanks to your love."

There were gifts exchanged among the others.

The afternoon hurried by. And then the visitors began to depart.

Samantha had offered to spend one more night at the manse, so Josh and Katie walked together to the house they had rented. Josh had allowed Katie to pay the first month's rent but insisted that after that, he would pay.

They stepped inside. He closed the door with his foot and pulled her into his arms.

"Welcome home, Mrs. Kinsley."

She pressed her hand to his heart. "My home is here."

He kissed her. "I have good news."

"Better than this?"

"Nothing is better than this." He kissed her again. "But you might like to hear this. I have a job."

"Oh. But I was anticipating having you here all day, every day."

"Why that's just plain selfish. Do you want to know what I'm going to be doing?"

"Of course."

"Kade and Flora are adding on to their house and want me to help."

"Oh?'

"It's a secret for now, but Flora is going to have a baby in the spring."

"How nice." She thought a couple of the other sisters might have a special secret too.

"But that's not the best news. Kade has visited Stewart Kennedy, and the man told him he could use some help on the place. Said he was getting too old to be a good rancher. So, he's offered me a partnership in the ranch."

"What? Are you going to move out there?"

"Not just me, silly. We all are. As soon as we finish Kade's project, he and I are going to build a house for us. What do you think of that?" He kissed her nose.

She grabbed his lapels and pulled him in for a better kiss.

"I think we shall be very happy."

He nodded. "I agree. Though I can't imagine being any happier than I am right now."

But she knew their happiness and joy would grow with each passing day. She had learned it was possible to trust again—to trust both God and man.

DEAR READER

Thank you for reading CHRISTMAS BRIDE.

I often choose books based on reviews. If you liked this book or have comments would you please go to Amazon and leave a review so others can find it?

If you've enjoyed this story, and would like to read more of Linda's books, you can learn more about upcoming releases by signing up for her newsletter. You will also be able to download a free book, *Cowboy to the Rescue*. Click here to sign up.

Connect with Linda online:

Website | Facebook | Join my email newsletter

ALSO BY LINDA FORD

Buffalo Gals of Bonners Ferry series

Glory and the Rawhide Preacher

Mandy and the Missouri Man

Joanna and the Footloose Cowboy

Circle A Cowboys series

Dillon

Mike

Noah

Adam

Sam

Pete

Austin

Romancing the West

Jake's Honor

Cash's Promise

Blaze's Hope

Levi's Blessing

A Heart's Yearning

A Heart's Blessing

A Heart's Delight

A Heart's Promise

Glory, Montana - the Preacher's Daughters

Loving a Rebel

A Love to Cherish

Renewing Love

A Love to Have and Hold

Glory, Montana - The Cowboys

Cowboy Father

Cowboy Groom

Cowboy Preacher

Glory, Montana - Frontier Brides

Rancher's Bride

Hunter's Bride

Christmas Bride

Wagon Train Romance series

Wagon Train Baby

Wagon Train Wedding

Wagon Train Matchmaker

Wagon Train Christmas

Renewed Love

Rescued Love

Reluctant Love

Redeemed Love

Dakota Brides series

Temporary Bride

Abandoned Bride

Second-Chance Bride

Reluctant Bride

Prairie Brides series

Lizzie

Maryelle

Irene

Grace

Wild Rose Country

Crane's Bride

Hannah's Dream

Chastity's Angel

Cowboy Bodyguard

Printed in Great Britain
by Amazon

26506738R00128